The Big Lie

If I kept a journal, I would have recorded that fifteen, the year things were supposed to get better, was the year I uncovered the Big Lie. Big Lies are myths made up by grown-ups. Peel away the soft, fluffy outer shell of these myths and you find a hard grain of truth.

The first Big Lie I unmasked was about love, that even if you love someone, there's no guarantee he will love you back. The second Big Lie concerned the old adage that when you have your tonsils removed, you can have all the ice cream you want.

**Other Apple Paperbacks
you will enjoy:**

FIFTEEN AT LAST

Candice F. Ransom

AN
APPLE
PAPERBACK

SCHOLASTIC INC.
New York Toronto London Auckland Sydney

*For Pat, whose fifteenth year was
certainly a lot more exciting than mine.*

ISBN 0-590-43526-4

Copyright © 1987 by Candice F. Ransom. All rights reserved.
Published by Scholastic Inc. APPLE PAPERBACKS is a registered
trademark of Scholastic Inc.

12 11 10 9 8 7 6 5 4 3   9/8 0 1 2 3/9

Printed in the U.S.A.   01

Chapter 1

I guess it was just fate that I received the science book with the message in it.

My life is like that. I have been known to break open fortune cookies and find a blank piece of paper. Once a dog ran past a whole line of people to bite *me* on the ankle. My friend Gretchen said the dog probably didn't like my socks.

The science book with the message in it could have been handed to Gretchen, who was sitting next to me, or the kid behind me, or anyone, for that matter. But no, Mr. Chapman gave the book to me. As I said, all part of the design.

We were given our physical science textbooks a week after school started. The science books were used, but that was the only thing about Oakton High School that wasn't brand-new.

As soon as I got my book, I wrote my

name on the inside cover in the handwriting I had been practicing all summer. *Kobie Roberts*. The capital *K* and *R* were three times bigger than the rest of the letters in my name. It was a signature befitting an up-and-coming artist whose career was held back only because she had to finish the last three years of high school.

Actually it was kind of nice being a sophomore (anything was better than groveling at the bottom of the heap as a freshman), and nicer still to be going to Oakton High. Compared to Woodson, the school I went to last year, Oakton was like Disneyland. Woodson was crowded, beat up, swarming with seniors, and dangerous to kids who weighed ninety-five pounds, like me.

Oakton was so new, the freshly painted white walls glared off the banks of shiny metal lockers, and you could see your reflection in the polished floors. Even better, there were no seniors. Since Oakton's student body was made up entirely of kids transferred from existing schools, seniors were allowed to graduate from their old schools. Instead of being next to the bottom of the heap, sophomores were in the middle, closest in line to the juniors, who would rule Oakton.

Nothing will go wrong this year, I thought, *now that my best friend is sitting beside me.* If that doesn't sound like any great feat, let me tell you that the two years Gretchen and I were separated were the worst I'd ever had. Woodson is still buzzing over the day a crackpot freshman practically got herself murdered. If Gretchen had been there, none of those awful things would have happened, and anyway, I'm not *really* a crackpot.

Gretchen Farris has been my best friend since second grade. We shared classes at Centreville Elementary, and seventh grade at Robert Frost Intermediate, and life was peachy-keen. But in our eighth grade year at Frost, life became inky-stinky. Gretchen was rushed into the "in-crowd," while her unpopular best friend withered on the sidelines. Then Gretchen was in an automobile accident that kept her out of school most of the year. She had a head injury and a terrible scar that was later fixed with plastic surgery. But because Gretchen had lost so much time, she had to repeat the eighth grade and I went on to Woodson High to suffer my freshman year. Through summer school and a lot of hard work, Gretchen managed to catch up. Now we were in tenth grade, in the same school, and even in some of the same classes, where we belonged.

And I was fifteen, at last. Last year, when I was having such a terrible time, my mother promised me things would definitely get better after I turned fifteen.

This *would* be the best year ever, I decided. But that was before I opened my science book.

Gretchen leaned over and whispered. "What do you think of orange and black and tigers?"

I looked at the mimeographed sheet she pushed across the table at me. Oakton High was like a volcanic island that had sprung up in the ocean overnight, without history or traditions. We were supposed to choose our own school colors and the school mascot.

"They do go together," I said. "But orange and black make me think of Halloween."

"What did you put?"

I hauled out a grubby paper from my notebook. "I was tempted to put turquoise and lime-green." Those were my favorite colors. "But turquoise and lime-green might be too distracting on the football field. So I picked royal blue and gold. And an alligator for a mascot."

"An alligator!" Gretchen exclaimed. "Why an alligator?"

"Well, they're ferocious and mean if you get too close to them around dinnertime. What's wrong with an alligator mascot?"

"Kobie, alligators live down south, in

Florida. We live in *Virginia,* northern Virginia, at that. The mascot should be an animal we can identify with."

"And how many tigers do you see prowling around Fairfax?" I countered.

"You know what I mean." Gretchen flipped her strawberry-blonde hair over one shoulder. She had let her hair grow over the summer and it fell in soft waves halfway down her back.

After a disastrous session with the scissors last year, in an attempt to give myself a Vidal Sassoon geometric haircut, I wound up instead with a half inch of hair that looked singed. My hair was now down to my chin, a respectable but boring length. All the girls in Oakton had long, long hair.

"I'll change my mascot if you change yours," Gretchen said, doubtful over her choice.

"Okay." I erased "alligator" and wrote in "skunk." "How's this? It's an animal native to our region."

Gretchen started giggling. I snatched up my physical science book and buried my face in it to keep from laughing. Mr. Chapman had let us pair off as lab partners, and I didn't want to risk our position by messing around in class too soon.

The page that I randomly opened to, a bunch of chemical equations, had been defaced with a big red heart inside which "I love Mike" had been scrawled. That was the trouble with used books. In the English book issued to me last year, some kid had underlined all the words beginning with "t" and drawn eyes in every double "o." I found myself stressing words beginning with "t," even when I talked, and coming across "boot" or "look" made me feel as if I were being watched.

I turned the page. "I love Mike" was blazoned across the end of the chapter questions and on the first page of the next chapter. I riffled the pages impatiently. On *every single page* some dippy girl had proclaimed her devotion to Mike. It was like snooping in somebody's diary.

I was about to raise my hand and request another book when I saw it. On page 289. *I love Mike still as in forever till there is no end.*

But on the page following that heartfelt vow, "Mike" had been ruthlessly crossed out and "Wayne" written under his name. Throughout the rest of the book, Wayne substituted for Mike, somehow canceling the declaration of undying love on page 289.

I had been thinking a lot about love lately. When I signed up for physical science, I hoped the class would clear up some of my questions. Judging from the book, physical science appeared to be a numbing combination of biology, physics, and chemistry, with absolutely nothing about love, unless you counted the previous book-owner's fickle vows.

What was love *really* like? Was it so powerful it caused a person to announce her feelings on every page of a textbook? And if love was so strong (as in *forever till there is no end*), then how could that girl have switched from one boy to another?

I nudged Gretchen to show her my book. She ignored the jab. Her round blue eyes were focused on a guy four tables over. Doug McNeil. He wasn't the cutest guy in class, but he had intense gray eyes and a slouchy, I-don't-care, James Dean kind of attitude. Gretchen was obviously attracted to him, and from the looks Doug was zinging back at her, the feeling was mutual.

"Gretch," I whispered. "Your chair is on fire."

No response.

"Gretch, a white mouse just ran over your foot. Didn't you feel his tail?"

Blue eyes continued to lock with gray.

I settled back in my seat with a sigh. That Gretchen had snared the interest of a boy was hardly earth-shattering. She had a great figure and a certain perkiness that most guys couldn't resist. Even as far back as eighth grade, Gretchen had boys falling over themselves. Last year, she'd been too self-conscious over her scar and too swamped with catch-up work to pay much attention to boys, but I could tell she was planning to make up for lost time.

As for me, there were no guys on the horizon.

The bell rang, snapping Gretchen out of her trance.

"See you later." She gathered her books in a hurry.

I caught her arm. "Gretch, what's with you and Doug McNeil?"

"Nothing," she said evasively. "I don't even know him."

"Maybe you ought to introduce yourselves before you stare holes through each other."

"Kobie, your imagination is working overtime again." But she held back just enough to walk out the door with Doug McNeil, leaving me to walk to French by myself. I felt a tremor in the air between us, like one of those unexplained ripples on the surface of a perfectly calm pond.

French class was just down the hall. As soon as I walked in the door a husky voice cried, "Kobie!"

"Stuart!" I shrieked back. Stuart and I always greeted each other like people reunited after twenty years on separate continents.

"Sit here, Kobie," Stuart insisted, patting the desk next to his and even dusting it off.

"Stuart, I've been sitting in that same chair a whole week now." I sat down.

"I want to make sure you don't *change* your seat."

Stuart Buckley and I had what novels called a "tumultuous relationship." I was friends with Stuart only because it was foolhardy to have him as an enemy. Stuart burst into my life like the stars you see when you are conked on the head. He was very short, wore thick glasses, and had a chip on his shoulder. Stuart resented his height and the fact that his new stepmother hated him. Even after his grandmother got custody of him (an act of great courage), he didn't settle down.

Mrs. Hildebrandt took attendance and then began writing on the board. As this was second-year French, I knew we would have our lessons conducted entirely in the language.

Stuart tipped his chair back on two legs and grinned at me. Mrs. Hildebrandt, who apparently had eyes in the back of her head, swiveled around and caught him. Stuart's chair hit the floor with a resounding *clunk*.

Dropping the chalk, the teacher said, *"Class, attention, s'il vous plaît."*

"Ici," Stuart said, in an accent straight

out of an old Charles Boyer movie. We all knew *ici* means "here." He extended his palm, as if offering Mrs. Hildebrandt an invisible bar of soap.

The other kids broke up. Mrs. Hildebrandt looked as if she wished she had gone to work in a torpedo factory instead of teaching.

I had never had Stuart in one of my classes before. He had been a locker neighbor, a lunch partner, someone to bump into in the halls — encounters highlighted by slamming, stealing, and bumming money, in that order. Now I understood why Stuart's teachers were reportedly seen gulping Tums and looking at the retirement schedule posted in the main office.

I wondered why Stuart felt it necessary to be so disruptive. Was he always this bad or was there a special reason for his showing off? And then I saw the reason.

Her name was Rosemary Swan.

Rosemary was smiling back at Stuart and he was blushing forty shades of red. My heart plummeted to the soles of my imitation Bass Weejuns. Rosemary Swan, a gorgeous girl with glossy black hair, snapping black eyes, and a shape that made me seethe with envy, was way out of Stuart's league. For one thing, she was nearly six feet tall. I knew, because Rosemary was in my gym class and we had all been weighed and measured last week. Stuart only came up to my shoulder and I barely stood five three.

"That girl up there," Stuart said, for once lowering his voice a decibel. "She thinks I'm funny. I bet she thinks I'm the funniest guy she's ever seen."

"Maybe," I conceded. "What do you care what she thinks?"

"Oh, I care," he said. The hope glowing on Stuart's face made me feel a little sick. First Gretchen and now Stuart!

This love business was getting more complicated by the minute. I was fifteen, not a kid anymore, yet already I felt years behind everyone else.

At home, I started to toss my books on the chair by the front door.

"In your room," my mother yelled from the kitchen. The woman has X-ray vision.

"Hello to you, too," I said.

"Hello," she added. "Don't forget to hang up your clothes, Kobie."

As if I could. In her determination to make her only daughter into a neater person, my mother had instituted an anti-slob campaign, directed at me. It was *hang up your clothes, don't throw your books around, pick up those papers* the second I opened my eyes in the morning, until I wearily closed them again at night.

I went into my room and took off my school outfit. This year, at least, I wasn't saddled with the ugliest clothes in the world. For my birthday this summer I got three skirts with matching blouses and sweaters, the Weejun lookalikes, and a genuine leather ring belt. If you didn't check the labels in my clothes, you'd never know I wasn't one of the cool "in" girls.

I hung up my skirt and blouse, which were too good to stuff in the pile of uglies I kept beside my dresser. From the pile, which my mother had been nagging me to get rid of for two years, I yanked out old corduroy jeans and a sweat shirt.

My room was actually shaping up okay, compared to the way it was last year. After pestering my mother to let me get a purple carpet, I finally convinced her that lime-green and turquoise were the best accent colors. We painted my filing cabinet turquoise and it really set the room off. Mom bought a fabric remnant in a turquoise and lime-green print and sewed new curtains. I still had my old, half-bald chenille bedspread, but it was hard to find bedspreads in turquoise.

Right before school started, Gretchen and I went shopping with our birthday cash (our birthdays are seven weeks apart) at the new mall at Tyson's Corner. I bought a turquoise and lime-green owl mobile, a set of felt pens, a record album by Bob Dylan, the folk singer, and a five-gallon aquarium.

The aquarium really made my room look cool. Sitting on top of my filing cabinet, it had turquoise foil on the back side, turquoise and lime-green mingled gravel in the bottom, a treasure chest that opened and closed with the action of the aerator, plastic plants, a diver, a ceramic castle, and a ceramic mermaid. My mother claimed the fish barely had room to wiggle through all that junk, but what did she know about marine life? We must have really crummy water because the four ungrateful fish I bought at Woolworth's all died within a week. Rather than invest in more fish, I just let the aquarium run empty.

My mother came into my room without knocking, a bad habit I was trying to get her to break.

"Mo-other!" I accused. "What if I'd been changing?"

"Oh, excuse me," she said with exaggerated politeness. "It isn't like I haven't seen you unclothed before. I used to change your diapers, remember." Only a mother would bring up another person's disgusting pre-toilet-trained days.

"Let's not talk about that," I said.

"Why not?" Mom lounged in the doorway and folded her arms. "You used to be such a cute little girl, Kobie. You had curly hair and fat, dimpled little legs . . . whenever I came to get you out of the crib you were so happy to see me."

The implication that I was no longer cute (the truth since my dimpled knees were now knobby and I Scotch-taped my hair to make it lie flat) made me testy. "Who wouldn't be happy? How would you like to be stuck in a crib until you're five years old? No wonder I'm underdeveloped."

"I couldn't trust you in a regular bed. You kept falling out on your head — "

"And that's what's wrong with me today," I finished for her.

"What's wrong with you today has nothing to do with your falling out of the crib," she said ominously.

"I know, I know. I'm a terrible, horrible, gruesome adolescent, and you wish I still had dimpled legs and dribbled Pablum all over the place." The trouble with mothers was that they couldn't face facts and let go of the past. I was fifteen, an *adult*.

"What do you want?" I asked.

"Nothing. Can't I come in to see you without a reason? How was school?"

"Okay."

"You act like you want to tell me something," she said. "What is it?"

I was dying to ask somebody knowledgeable about this love business but figured my own mother would be a bad candidate for two reasons: (a) she would automatically jump to the conclusion that I was carrying on in school instead of paying attention to my lessons, and (b) whatever she once knew about love had happened so long ago it would be like asking Rip Van Winkle what he did when he wasn't napping.

"Do we have any Ding Dongs left?" I said instead.

"You ate the last one yesterday and I haven't been to the store."

"How come whenever we run out of something dumb like coffee or milk you run up to the store in your bedroom slippers, but if I run out of goodies, I have to wait till next grocery day?"

"I do *not* go to the store in my bedroom slippers." As usual, my mother selected the least important part of my complaint to comment on. "You know, Kobie, Ding Dongs are not a right but a privilege. And privileges can be taken away."

I wanted to argue my rights, but it would have been self-defeating for an almost-adult, fifteen-year-old to take a strong stand over Ding Dongs.

"I'll fix you some peanut butter crackers," Mom said, letting me off the hook. "Are you going to draw?"

"Maybe later."

Stored in the turquoise filing cabinet was my latest art project, illustrations from the Walt Disney movie *Lady and the Tramp*. My ambition was to be an animator for Walt Disney Studios in Burbank, California. In the evenings after my homework was done, I would sketch scenes from a Golden Book version of the movie in India ink, and color them in with my new felt pens. I was very diligent about this project. By the time I graduated from Oakton, my portfolio would be so good, I'd be hired on the spot as an animator.

But today I wasn't in the mood for drawing. I flicked on my record player.

My mother immediately yelled from the hall, "You're not going to play that awful record, are you?" For some reason, my mother despised my new album. I played it every day. You'd think she'd be used to it.

I put the album on the spindle.

"Kobie, don't play that record!"

The tone arm settled into the grooves and the first song twanged out of the speaker. Down the hall, my mother slammed a door.

I opened my physical science book to the "Mike" message. I had a lot to think about.

Chapter 2

Right Things I Have:
1. *Three new outfits (A-line skirts, blouses, and matching cardigans)*
2. *Imitation Bass Weejun loafers*
3. *Genuine leather ring belt*
4. *Makeup: blush-on, mascara, eyeliner, lipgloss, "Iced Espresso" eyeshadow*

Right Things to Get:
1. *Real leather purse (lost cause)*
2. *Long hair (let grow)*
3. *Long fingernails (stop biting!)*

One morning in late September, I skimmed my "Right Things" list before leaving for school. Gretchen and I started a "Right Things" list last year, so we would know what things to buy or do in order to be popular. Gretchen didn't really need a list — she usually had the right things, and people just naturally liked her anyway.

Even if I had been born wearing a designer diaper, I'd have been snubbed in the sandbox by the popular babies.

But this year all that would change, I realized as I tallied both columns. On the plus side, I had the same clothes the other girls were wearing, and my mother, after a heated debate, had consented to let me wear makeup. Those two items were the most important.

I didn't have a real leather purse, it was true. My mother said she refused to mortgage the house to pay for one pocketbook. And my hair was definitely too short. I tossed my head to see if my hair was long enough to swirl the way Gretchen's did. Then I remembered to pull off the row of Scotch tape I had wound around the ends to keep my hair from curling. My fingernails were the worst, bitten past the quick and bristling with hangnails. Every year *Stop biting nails* was number one among my New Year's resolutions, but I couldn't quit for more than a day before I'd get a terrible nail-biting attack.

Still, the positive side of the list outweighed the minus side. One item on the plus side I hadn't included was Gretchen's influence. She would pull me into the popular crowd with her. Armed with the "right" things, all I had to do was wait for Barb Levister or Patty Binninger, two popular girls around whom cliques seemed to be forming, to ask me to sit with them at a pep rally or something. Maybe when I got on the bus today, Gretchen would announce that we had been invited to sit at Barb's library table during study hall.

"Bus in five minutes!" my mother called, rapping her spoon on the wall.

I pounded the wall back to let her know I was almost ready.

My bedroom was located next to the kitchen. Instead of getting up from the table and coming all the way in here to wake me up or to tell me to hurry, my mother merely leans over and raps on the wall with a butter knife or her coffee spoon. *Crackcrackcrack!* It certainly does the trick.

After slapping a handful of Ambush cologne on my neck, I clicked off my radio and grabbed my books. My mother was stationed by the front door to give me my lunch money and/or inspect me.

"Whew! Don't you think that cologne's a little strong for this early in the morning?"

"Oh, Mother! *Everybody* wears Ambush!"

"The boys, too?"

"Of course not. Boys wear Hai Karate or English Leather."

"Then I pity your poor teachers, facing

19

a whole reeking classroom every morning." She frowned and I knew what was coming next. "What's that stuff around your eyes?"

"Eyeliner. Mom, why do you start these discussions right before the bus? You told me *ages* ago I could wear makeup."

"Just because I said you could wear it doesn't mean I approve of your going to school looking like a raccoon with insomnia."

We stared at each other, the old mother-daughter-eyeball battle. I blinked first. The four coats of mascara I had applied in an effort to lengthen my stubby lashes until "they swept the floor" were making my eyes water. My mother must have thought I was going to cry, because she kissed my cheek and told me to run catch the bus.

Gretchen had saved our special seat, third from the front on the left. We had been sitting in that same seat for years.

"Boy, Mom was really on my case today," I told Gretchen. "According to her, I have on too much eyeliner and too much — "

"Kobie, guess what! You're not going to believe this!" Gretchen squealed before I was finished griping.

Excitement shivered down my spine. My dream was about to come true! After years of waiting to get into the popular crowd, I was about to hear we were now part of either Barb's or Patty's group. At last!

"Hurry and tell me! I'm dying!"

"Doug McNeil called last night and asked me out! This Friday — tomorrow! Kobie, isn't it the greatest?" Her blue eyes were shining.

"How did he get your phone number?" I asked, pulling my mother's annoying trick of picking the least important part of a shocking statement to comment on.

"He asked me for it in homeroom yesterday."

Gretchen and I were in three classes together: typing, gym, and physical science, the class where she and Doug made goo-goo eyes at each other. Clearly, things had progressed beyond the staring stage, and it had evidently happened in homeroom.

I pretended to be miffed. "How come you didn't tell me on the phone last night?"

"He called after we hung up. I would have called you right back, honest, Kobie, but it was late. You know how your mother is about phone calls after nine." She clutched my arm and gave it a joyful squeeze. "I can't wait till tomorrow! What do you think I should wear?"

"Are you allowed to date so soon?" I asked, trying not to let disappointment show in my voice. This sounded serious.

Gretchen had gone out with guys before, but only on a casual basis, like meeting them at a party or something. As for me, my mother's opinion about dating at fifteen was the same as getting phone calls after nine. In words of one syllable, *no!*

"Sure, I can go out," Gretchen replied breezily. "Kobie, you'll have to talk your mother into letting you date before sixteen. You'll find a guy and then the four of us can double."

Gretchen didn't seem to realize that I had wheedled my mother about as far as I could. I had talked her into letting me wear short skirts, stockings, makeup, buy a purple carpet she had no intention of buying, and keep a fish tank, even though there weren't any fish in it. But mothers are like mules; they can only be pushed to a point and then they balk.

"You'd better forget about doubling for a while," I said. "With me, anyway. Besides, you haven't even gone out once with Doug. You might hate him after Friday night."

"No, I won't." Gretchen looked at me with a new grown-up confidence, and I wondered how the seven weeks between our birthdays could make such a difference. "Kobie, I think this is *it*. Doug is the one."

"The one what?"

She poked me in the ribs. "The *one. The* one. You know."

"Oh, yeah. The one." *As in forever till there is no end.* "Gretch, how do you *know* Doug's the one?"

"I just do." She smiled slyly. "When it happens to you, Kobie, you'll know, too."

Easy for her to say. Unless I became skilled with a lasso, there was no chance of my getting near a boy long enough to find out if he was *it* or not. Why did Gretchen have to stir up this boy stuff before I was ready? Why couldn't she have been satisfied with buying the "right" things and hanging out with the "right" crowd? She always had to be a jump ahead of me.

I had another item to add to my "Right Things to Get" list: *Number four. A boyfriend.*

Thanks to Sandy Robertson, I was the only person in the history of W.T. Woodson High School — maybe even the state of Virginia — to have almost been murdered in the parking lot during D lunch shift. Separated from Gretchen, I had let myself fall into the wrong company last year. It wasn't hard.

Robertson comes from right after Roberts and this Robertson in particular turned up like a bad penny in three of my alphabetically organized classes. Sandy and I shared a locker and nearly shared a jail cell before the first semester was over.

Sandy had green eyes, a cute smile, taffy-blonde hair, and a slight limp because she'd had polio when she was very young and refused to wear the built-up orthopedic shoe that corrected her hip displacement. She also attracted trouble like a lightning rod.

It was Sandy who angered Jeanette Adams, but it was *me* Jeanette threatened to murder in the parking lot. Obviously Jeanette Adams did not kill me, but one crazy afternoon, during which I ran to the police and was then brought back to school in a squad car while Sandy hunted for my crumpled body under the cars and my mother sobbed in my guidance counselor's office, was enough to permanently stamp me as "weirdo" at Woodson.

My reputation at Woodson was in tatters, but I stood a better-than-fair chance at Oakton, where everyone was new and reputations, even weird ones, had been left behind. Unfortunately, Sandy Robertson had *not* been left behind.

Sandy wasn't a bad kid, really. She meant well and she was actually fun to be around, if you had nerves of flint. Last summer I introduced Sandy and Gretchen, hoping they would hit it off since it appeared I would be burdened with Sandy as long as there were "R"s in the alphabet. Just as I had hoped, they got along fine. Gretchen had a soothing influence on Sandy, but whenever it was just me and Sandy, Sandy tended to go out of bounds. This year Sandy was in my "dummy" math class, as well as English, gym, and the same lunch shift.

By lunchtime, I was in no mood for Sandy or Stuart or anybody. In first period typing, all Gretchen did was rhapsodize over Doug. Doug this. Doug that. How gorgeous she thought Doug was.

Between English and gym, I saw Gretchen and Doug lingering by her locker. She never even heard me when I yelled hello. As I trudged through the food line, I had a not-very-nice-but-typical-Kobie thought: Maybe Gretchen would have a rotten time with Doug and then we could go back to our original goal — getting into the right group.

Sandy had saved me a seat in the cafeteria. "I bet I did terrible on that English quiz," she said, as I sat down with my tray.

"Me, too." Miss Boyes was turning out to be one of those teachers who felt obligated to pop a quiz every other day.

"Not you. You probably got an A, like always."

Sandy had a short memory. Last year, I flat-out flunked — as in *failed* — home ec and gym, the two classes I had with Sandy and Jeanette Adams, the gangster who masqueraded as a freshman. I usually did okay in most subjects, as long as no one was gunning for me.

The spiral notebook Sandy used for English had the name "Cassandra Robertson" on the cover.

"I didn't know your name is really Cassandra," I said.

"It isn't. I don't like Sandy anymore. It's so ordinary." She pointed to my notebook. "I'm practicing to write my name fancy like you do. Your signature looks so neat. I wish I had a 'K' in my name." Grubbing for a pencil in her purse, she scrawled, *Kassandra Robertson.* "What do you think?"

"I think it's dumb. What's wrong with Sandy?"

"Fingernail check," Sandy announced.

I held out my hands, splaying my fingers so she could examine my nails. "You don't need to squint so. They haven't grown any."

"I think they have. I can almost feel the edge of your thumbnail."

"That's the one I chewed in English this morning."

She wouldn't give up. "You only chewed

it a little. It definitely looks longer than it did yesterday."

The thing about Sandy was that she wanted to be just like me. *Exactly* like me. When I told her I wanted to grow my nails, she gnawed off all her own fingernails — *perfectly good* fingernails — so we could grow our nails together. She followed me around like a cocker spaniel, imitating every aspect of my mostly dull life, forever telling me how smart I was, how well I could draw, how good I looked.

Next to Sandy, I did look pretty good, not because I thought I should be Miss America, but because Sandy always looked like she lived in a bus terminal.

Gretchen and I were alike in lots of ways, but we didn't want to be Siamese twins. Sandy was more an appendage than a friend. I learned long ago that it was easier to remove flypaper welded to the sole of my shoe than get rid of Sandy.

Today, though, Sandy's attentions were welcome, after Gretchen's unending fascination with Doug McNeil.

"Are you having corned beef hash and canned peas for supper tomorrow night?" Sandy asked.

My parents ate a late supper on Fridays, so my mother fixed me whatever I wanted on that night. When Sandy found out I ate corned beef hash and canned peas every single Friday night, she made her mother fix that, too. I'm sure the Robertsons are sick of corned beef hash and peas.

"I don't have hash and peas anymore," I said. "Now it's homemade pizza with bacon, an RC, and a pack of Suzy-Q's." My mother, I knew, was hoping that this Friday night obsession would fade. She grumbled every week about the chore of rolling out pizza dough *extra-thin* and frying up bacon *extra-crispy* to suit my picky tastes.

Sandy dropped her fork with an indignant clatter. "You didn't tell me!" she cried, outraged. "You didn't tell me you changed the menu! What kind of pizza mix? In a round pan or a square one?"

I responded to her questions, thinking that Mrs. Robertson would soon have her hands in sticky pizza dough, hands she would rather wrap around my neck. "Sandy, you don't have to eat the same thing I do," I told her. "Come up with your own Friday night supper."

"I like doing what you do," Sandy said. "You do everything just right, Kobie. Anyway, if we eat the same thing, it's kind of like being together on Friday nights, isn't it?"

All this talk about Friday night reminded me of Gretchen's upcoming date with Doug. "We shouldn't be sitting home eating pizza," I said. "We ought to be going out. On real dates. Are you allowed to date yet?"

"Sure," Sandy replied, surprising me. I thought her mother was as behind the times as mine was. "If anybody asks me out, I can go."

"Your mother would let you?"

Sandy shrugged. "She doesn't care. After raising three girls, she's used to dating." Sandy had three older sisters, all married. "Linda, my oldest sister, says Mom got more easygoing with each of us. Now that there's just me, she's practically putty in my hands."

The day my mother becomes putty will be the day the earth orbits too close to the sun. Even if I'd had an army of older sisters, my mother would still be plaster-of-paris stubborn when it came to letting me date.

"Has some guy asked you out?"

"No." I tasted the bread pudding, then pushed the dish away. "And no one will, either."

"How can you say that? You're really cute, Kobie. You're always putting yourself down."

"I'm too skinny," I said. "Boys don't like skinny girls. That's why I eat all that junk on Fridays. To gain weight."

"What about that boy down there? He's

been staring at you ever since you sat down. I bet *he* likes you. He must, to keep looking at you that way."

I followed her gaze. A chunky boy in a blue sweater was sitting at the end of our table, all by himself. His English book was open before him, but he was staring at me. When he caught me looking back, he smiled shyly.

"He does like you!" Sandy cried. "He's crazy about you, anybody can see it! That boy really likes you!"

"That's no boy," I said dismally. "That's Eddie Showalter."

"What do you mean, that's no boy?"

"I mean, it's Eddie Showalter. He doesn't count."

He didn't, believe me. At least not in the pool of boys I would consider dating. I knew Eddie Showalter from ninth grade geography. Eddie was noted for wearing the same sweater every day, no matter what the weather, and for drawing cartoons of the White House and jet airplanes in the margins of his textbook. Despite the color change in his sweater today and a nice kind of pudginess, Eddie Showalter had not vastly improved over the summer. There wasn't anything terribly *wrong* with Eddie, but there wasn't anything quite *right* about him, either.

"I think he's cute," Sandy said. "He's

got big brown eyes like yours. You both look like Lassie."

"Maybe we should get married and start a kennel," I said dryly.

Gretchen's date tomorrow night with Doug McNeil was only the beginning, I sensed. After all, Gretchen claimed Doug was *it*. *It* also described Eddie Showalter and Stuart Buckley, the only boys I knew, but the two situations couldn't be compared in the same breath. If I didn't want Gretchen to get too far ahead of me, I would have to get myself a boyfriend, one who didn't mind that I was skinny, couldn't talk on the phone after nine o'clock, and would be content with an at-school relationship.

Glancing over at Eddie, I rejected the possibility of going out with either him or Stuart. And since all the other boys in Oakton — who were more interested in types like Rosemary Swan — had already rejected *me*, I would have to look elsewhere.

Chapter 3

"And while we were eating French fries in the Pot O'Gold, he asked me if I'd be his girl. I said yes. I didn't even have to think about it, Kobie. I've known all along I wanted to be Doug's girl. Then he took off this ring and gave it to me. He said, 'Now that you're my girl, I want you to wear this. Promise me you'll be mine, always.' Isn't that the most *romantic* thing you ever heard?"

"Mmmmm," I replied vaguely. Gretchen told her story without missing a beat on her typing exercise, but I had just discovered that my right pinky finger did not reach the backspace key like it was supposed to.

"Isn't it a beautiful ring?" Gretchen asked. She stopped typing long enough to flourish the gold ring with the onyx stone she was wearing on a chain around her neck. "When we order our class rings later this year, I'm ordering what Doug wants and he's ordering what I want, since we'll exchange rings as soon as we get them."

I thought that arrangement was like two people building a house before they were formally engaged, but I said nothing. It was hard to get a word in edgewise. Gretchen had never been so talkative, so full of herself. Since Sunday night I had heard her saga — a love story to rival Cleopatra and Marc Antony — five times, and it was only first period Monday morning.

She called me Saturday morning before anyone in my house had gotten out of bed to report, in breathless detail, how wonderful her date Friday night had been with Mr. Magnificent. So wonderful that Doug was taking her to the mall on Sunday afternoon. Sunday night she called with the news that Doug had asked her to be his girl and had given her his ring. Then she called later, after she had talked to Doug to say *he* had called, and then she called me a *third* time to tell me the story *again*. I listened to her again on the bus this morning, my eyes glazing over, and once more in typing. I fully expected to look in the mirror and see the account of Gretchen's date etched across my forehead.

"Gretchen, are you sure you aren't rushing into things?" I asked, finally figuring out that I would have to raise my right hand off the keyboard in order to backspace. According to Mrs. Antle, our teacher, this method of typing had been designed so that a person's fingers would never have to leave the keyboard. I needed to find a method that compensated for midget fingers.

"I mean, you've only had two dates," I went on. "Before you start singing 'Oh Promise Me,' shouldn't you get to know Doug better?"

Gretchen stared at me. "Kobie, I *do* know Doug. How many dates we have doesn't matter. We both knew from the beginning that we were made for each other."

I lifted my eyes from my copy stand to look at her. If ever a person was in love it was Gretchen. She positively radiated happiness. As for me, I had a splitting headache, caused by either thirty clattering typewriters or the knowledge that Gretchen had taken another giant step away from me.

Ever since we both turned thirteen, I had been running to keep up with her. Gretchen was allowed to wear stockings before I was, and have her ears pierced, and stuff like that, but her pulling away from me was more than just getting

34

grown-up things. I pictured entering adult-
hood as passing through a haze-shrouded
doorway. I could see the door but my feet
were dragging. Gretchen was halfway
through to the other side. Pretty soon she'd
be out of my sight.

"Eyes on your work, girls," Mrs. Antle
said, making one of her frequent circuits
behind our chairs to watch us.

Gretchen looked away first and resumed
typing. I noticed her pinky finger had no
trouble at all reaching the backspace key.

By lunchtime my headache was worse
and my throat felt scratchy besides. I took
my tray over to our regular table. Sandy
Robertson wasn't holding a seat for me, but
Eddie Showalter was.

He smiled as I sat down. "Hi, Kobie."

"Hi." I searched the area for Sandy,
thinking maybe she had switched tables.
She wasn't anywhere to be seen. I un-
zipped my straw wrapper and stabbed it
into my milk carton. "Aren't you eating?"
I asked Eddie.

He shook his head. "Naw. I never eat
lunch." He must have made up for it at
dinner, since he was on the chunky side.

Still, I felt guilty eating in front of him.
"Are you sure you don't want a bite? Part
of my macaroni or something?"

"No, thanks. I got your note. What did you want?"

I nearly choked on a spoonful of applesauce. "What note?"

"The note you sent me."

I had not, under any circumstances, sent a note to Eddie Showalter. I had nothing to say to Eddie Showalter, either verbally or in written form. There must be some mistake. "I sent you a note?"

"Don't you remember?" Eddie's thick, wiggly eyebrows shot upward. "I found it in my locker right before third. And it was definitely from you."

I rubbed my forehead, which felt hot and dry.

"Are you okay, Kobie?" Eddie sounded concerned.

No, I was not. Gretchen was going steady, which meant I could forget about her helping me get into the in-crowd, my little finger was at least an inch too short, and I had apparently written a note to a boy I didn't particularly like, asking him who-knew-what.

"You might as well know the truth, Eddie. I have this — condition. It's called . . . note amnesia."

"Note amnesia?" He didn't sound the least bit convinced, but I plunged ahead anyway.

"Yeah. See, sometimes I write notes to people, but I forget about it as soon as I've delivered the note. It's sort of like when people sleepwalk and do things that later they don't remember doing? Well, when I write notes, it's instantly zapped from my memory. Just exactly what did I *say* in my note?"

"I've got it right here." Eddie produced a much-crumpled sheet of notebook paper.

Dear Eddie, the note said in an experimental backslanted handwriting I immediately recognized as belonging to a certain green-eyed blonde who would have to learn to write with her other hand by the time I got done with her. *Please meet me at lunch at the end of the table I saw you sitting at the other day. I have something to ask you.*

"Do you remember what you wanted to ask me?" Eddie asked in a careful tone.

"Yes," I said before I could think properly. "It's about that homework assignment we got today. I don't understand it."

"What homework assignment?"

"You know, in the class we have together." I knew Eddie and I shared a class but I was too rattled to remember which one.

"Kobie, we're in *homeroom* together."

"Oh. Well, that was some roll-call Mrs. Wade gave today, wasn't it?"

Mercifully he changed the subject, rescuing me from a poor recovery. "How do you like Oakton?"

"After Woodson? It's great. But weren't we supposed to get a students' lounge with Coke machines?"

"I heard that same rumor, but only the teachers have a lounge. We do have a planetarium," he added, as if he'd been elected a one-man Oakton High School Chamber of Commerce.

"We had a planetarium at Woodson," I said. "A lot of good it did us. Only little kids on field trips got to use it."

Eddie nodded. "I went to the planetarium when I was in seventh grade."

"Me, too. When I was at Frost. Did you go to Lanier?" Sandy Robertson had gone to Sidney Lanier Intermediate. I was wondering how she was connected with Eddie. Also how I'd keep from choking her when I saw her again.

"No, I went to Poe," Eddie replied.

What an exciting conversation. Planetariums and old intermediate schools. Next thing, we'd be talking about who we pushed on the swings. How had Gretchen managed to advance beyond idiot remarks like these to an onyx ring around her neck? Then I remembered the way she and Doug stared at each other in science class. Love had nothing to do with *talking*, it was all in the *eyes*. I looked into Eddie's, then glanced away, embarrassed. His eyes were brown, like mine. Looking at him was too much like gazing into a mirror.

Whatever had happened to Gretchen and Doug would never happen to Eddie Showalter and me. No meaningful looks passed between us, no electricity sparked the air over my half-eaten macaroni and cheese.

My last class was "dummy" math, actually Algebra I, Part II. Because my feeble brain couldn't take first-year algebra in a single dose, I opted for the two-year watered-down version. The class was held in the industrial arts wing, where kids took shop and mechanical drawing and the math dummies wouldn't contaminate the smart kids.

Sandy Robertson was in algebra with me. I was most anxious to see her, despite the fact that I was feeling awful. Sandy's lunchtime matchmaking scheme was fairly mild compared to the escapades she got me into last year, but I suspected this little thing with Eddie was just a warm-up exercise.

Though the late bell had rung, my math teacher was outside the classroom, deep in conversation with another teacher. Sandy was standing boldly on the other side of the doorway, waiting for me.

"How did it go with you and Eddie?" she asked.

"How did you think it went?" I replied. "What possessed you to write that note? I felt like a fool when he asked me what I wanted."

Sandy was unconcerned. "I knew you'd come up with something. You always do. At least you and Eddie were alone together, thanks to me. He really likes you, Kobie."

"Thanks to you, he probably thinks I'm crazy. Anyway, even if he does like me, I'm not so sure I like *him*."

"Yes, you do," she persisted. "You just don't know it. If I tell you your fortune, will you believe it then?"

"Only if it is written in the stars that a certain nosy girl will butt out." I rubbed my eyes again. My face felt taut and shiny, like the skin on an eggplant. Every time I swallowed, my throat hurt. Maybe I was coming down with the flu . . . or a virus. I wanted to go home, but I had one more class.

"Let's go inside," I said. Mr. Bell was still talking to the other teacher. The second teacher had his back to us, which meant that Mr. Bell could look over and spot us any minute.

And he did. He called over the other teacher's shoulder. "Girls. You belong inside."

The teacher he had been talking to turned around to see who had interrupted their conversation.

I gulped. The other teacher was young and drop-dead gorgeous. He had light brown hair, cut very short, as if he played a lot of sports and didn't want to mess with long hair in the shower; and blue eyes, the bluest eyes I had ever seen. No, not ordinary blue, *turquoise!*

He stared at me with his beautiful turquoise eyes. I couldn't tear my own eyes away. Electricity sizzled between us. We could have lit up the whole county with the energy we were generating.

My face was on fire, my throat like a branding iron. But it wasn't the flu or a virus at all . . . I had fallen in love!

Chapter 4

"Tonsillitis," the doctor diagnosed, retrieving what felt like a two-foot-long tongue depressor from my mouth.

"Does that mean she has bad tonsils?" my mother asked.

"They're pretty rotten, all right," the doctor replied cheerfully, scribbling on a prescription pad.

I wasn't even insulted. My throat hurt, but I hardly noticed, my thoughts were so full of the Man with the Turquoise Eyes. One minute I was stunned by this man in the hall outside my math class, the next I was in Dr. Wampler's office undergoing an examination. How could a person fall in love and get tonsillitis at the same time?

"They'll have to come out," the doctor said. With a shudder I realized he meant my tonsils.

"It's so early in the school year," my

mother murmured. "Can it wait until summer?"

Dr. Wampler had red hair and freckles. He was young, for a doctor, and he winked at me as he tore off the prescription and gave it to my mother. "Okay, ladies, here's the scoop. Kobie's tonsillitis isn't serious, but it's probably going to be chronic until she has those tonsils removed. This antibiotic will clear up her infection in a few days, but every time she gets run down or has a cold, you can expect another seige."

My mother looked distraught but not half as distraught as *I* must have looked. After all, they were talking about *my* tonsils, not hers.

"If she has the operation, will she miss much school?" My mother gets totally upset if I miss more than five minutes per semester per grade, afraid I'll turn out to be a dumb bunny or a juvenile delinquent or both.

"Kobie is fifteen, by medical standards, an adult." I sat up straighter, delighted to be recognized as an adult at last, if only by a surgeon who couldn't wait to operate on me. Dr. Wampler continued, "She'll only be in the hospital overnight, barring complications, but her recuperation period at home could vary. It's difficult to say how much time she'd lose."

"We'll wait," my mother decided. "It would be better for her to have the operation in the summer."

It wasn't until I was tucked in bed with a new issue of *Tiger Beat* and a big glass of juice on my nightstand that the impact of Dr. Wampler's diagnosis hit home. Tonsillitis! I had *tonsillitis*, a disease only *children* got. Tonsillitis was for *babies*. How could I, a fifteen-year-old *adult*, come down with such a degrading condition? This was as bad as getting measles or chicken pox. Why couldn't I have something respectable, like mono?

One good thing about staying home sick was that Gretchen would miss me at school. She'd call the second she got off the bus, in a lather of worry over me. I lay back on my pillows, making little hurty sounds every time I swallowed (this was for the benefit of my mother, who fluttered around my door because I was missing one whole day of school) and thought about Turquoise Eyes.

He had to be the handsomest man at Oakton High, maybe even the world. It was no coincidence that his eyes were my favorite color. As Sandy would say, it was Fate. He had been lightning-struck, too, that was apparent. Something had definitely happened between us those few powerful seconds we stared at each other.

"Feeling better?" my mother asked for the two hundredth time that afternoon, intent on saving me from possible ruin by sending me back to school as soon as I lumbered to my feet, like an old workhorse.

I almost told her "no," but actually the medicine was making me feel better, and anyway, I had to get back and see Turquoise Eyes again. "I think I'm okay. I can probably go to school tomorrow," I said, amazing my mother.

"We don't want to rush things," she said, contrarily. "Maybe you ought to stay in another day."

I flopped on the mattress, sweaty and petulant. "I *have* to go to school tomorrow. I have a big French test." I had no such thing but I couldn't stand the thought of being away from Turquoise Eyes another twenty-four hours.

My mother narrowed her eyes. "We'll see. You can make up the test. Your teacher will understand if you're sick." She left to make me creamed potato soup for supper.

Four o'clock came and went and Gretchen did not call. At four-thirty I got up and padded out to the phone. Gretchen's line was busy. It was busy at four thirty-seven and still busy at four forty-nine. She was probably yakking to Doug when she should have been inquiring after my health . . . I dialed her number the umpteenth time. This time it rang.

Gretchen's mother answered. "I'm sorry, Kobie, Gretchen isn't here. Charles picked her and Doug up after school and took them to that new miniature golf place in Annandale."

Dating during the school week yet! Why didn't Gretchen and Doug just announce their engagement and get it over with? She knew I wasn't in school and yet she hadn't even bothered to call! There was something indecent about a person out with a boy, hitting a little white ball through a fake windmill, while her best friend tottered at death's door.

The phone rang before I got back into bed. It was Sandy.

"You weren't in school today!" She nearly pierced my eardrum. "What's wrong?"

"I'm sick," I whined. At last, *somebody* cared.

"Poor Kobie! What've you got? The flu?"

"No, it's — " I stopped myself just in time. No way would I reveal to the general public that I had a little kid's disease. If I told Sandy I had tonsillitis, I might as well print it on the front page of the *Washington Post*. "It's nothing," I amended. "Just a sore throat."

"Those can be real awful. Anything I

can do for you while you're out?"

Having a second-best friend, even one as questionable as Sandy, had its merits. At least *she* wasn't whooping it up on a miniature golf course. "I'll probably be back day after tomorrow. But there is one thing you can do for me."

"Name it."

"You know that teacher Mr. Bell was talking to yesterday? When we were out in the hall? Find out who he is."

Gretchen did call later, but I was asleep. My mother kept me home the next day, overriding my loud protests that I was well enough to go to school. My temperature was down, but she claimed I might have a relapse or something. Now if I hadn't *wanted* to go to school, she would have propped me up at the bus stop on crutches, forcing me to adhere to the Virginia state law that every child shall receive an education.

I was grumpy by late afternoon when my mother told me Gretchen was on the phone.

"Talk an hour," she said, clearly at her wit's end. "Talk all night if you want. Be sure and tell her what a big baby you've been the past two days."

"You'll be sorry when I'm gone," I said, taking the receiver. "Gretchen?" I made my voice faint and scratchy, like my father's old 78 records.

"Kobie?" Gretchen said anxiously. "What's wrong? I called you last night but you were already in bed."

"That's because *some* people are too sick to stay up waiting for *other* people to get back from a date. How's your golf game these days?"

"I knew you'd be mad. Sorry I didn't call earlier. When Doug asked me to play miniature golf, I only had time to make arrangements with my mother and Charles." Charles, her older brother, had a car and was often pressed into service to taxi Gretchen around. "Kobie, what *is* the matter? I've been worried."

"You have?" Despite her recent thoughtlessness because of a mere boy, Gretchen Farris was still my best friend. "I've got tonsillitis. I have to have my tonsils out next summer. Don't you dare laugh! Gretch, promise you won't tell anybody?"

"Not even Doug?"

"Doug! Why would he care whether my tonsils were rotten or not?"

"We don't have any secrets. I tell Doug everything."

"You mean, you blab stuff that happened to you and me?" I could imagine their date the other day.

"Well, not so much about you," she admitted reluctantly. "We haven't gotten to that stage yet."

"What stage?" Gretchen's love life was, if nothing else, a great way to forget about a sore throat. Plus, I needed all this information. Sooner or later — maybe tomorrow! — Turquoise Eyes would declare his feelings for me and I had to be prepared for all the stages that come after that.

"See, we're still finding out about each other. We talk about personal stuff. Our childhoods, things like that. Doug wants to know every detail about when I was a little girl. When we're done with our pasts, we'll start in on our friends."

"Oh, really? And which chapter in your autobiography do I come in?" I didn't know how Gretchen could spend three entire dates with a guy talking about herself and never once mentioning me, her best friend.

Gretchen giggled. "Kobie, you're so funny."

"Yeah, that's me. Funny old Kobie." Time I quit clowning and let Gretchen know I had caught up to her, almost. She wasn't the only sophomore girl in Oakton to fall in love. "Listen, Gretch, I've got something really important to tell you on the bus tomorrow."

"Why not now?"

"The pho-ne," I said, singsonging the word to let her know my mother was hovering in the vicinity.

The next morning it was pouring. My mother drove me to school so I wouldn't have to wait for the bus in the rain. I didn't see Gretchen until first-period typing.

"What is this important thing you have to tell me?" she asked, adjusting Doug's ring so it wouldn't clank against the metal edge of her typewriter.

"I'm in love," I blurted. "Just like you."

"In love!" Gretchen gasped. "With who? Anybody I know?"

"I don't think so. He's new here this year."

"We're *all* new at Oakton," Gretchen pointed out.

"I mean, he's not anybody you'd know from our old schools." I fiddled with the carriage return lever.

"Kobie, will you spit it out? What's he look like? What's his name?"

"His name is — well, I call him Turquoise Eyes. T.E., for short." I liked the idea of my true love having a nickname.

"Turquoise Eyes? What kind of a name is that?" She frowned, probably thinking I was making him up.

"I don't know his real name yet," I said in a rush. "I'm still working on that. But he's absolutely gorgeous! Tall, light brown hair, and the bluest eyes you've ever seen. Not blue like yours, but turquoise. That's why I call him T.E."

"How come you don't know his name? Is he a junior?"

"Not exactly," I hedged. "But he *is* older than me." As soon as she found out T.E. was a teacher, she'd really tease me.

Gretchen thought out loud. "If he's not a junior and he's not a sophomore, he sure wouldn't be a freshman. He can't be a senior because there aren't any. That only leaves — " She stared at me. "Kobie, you're not talking about a *teacher*, are you?"

"Yes, but it's not what you think. He's interested in me, too. We had one of those stages you and Doug went through — you know, with the eyes? When we looked at each other, it was just like you described. I knew he was *it*. This isn't one of those dopey teacher-crush deals. This is *real*."

"But, Kobie, a teacher!" She shook her head. "Does *he* know this is it?"

"He must! Gretch, when our eyes met, it was — like lightning! He'd have to know." In my excitement to recreate the moment for her, I forgot my typing drill. "The walls and floors disappeared and there was nothing but him and me ... and electricity! The air practically crackled between us. We just kept staring at each other. That was *it*, all right."

Gretchen was still doubtful. "You don't even know his name — he doesn't know *your* name."

Her doubtfulness was wearing thin. Simply because she had Doug's ring around her neck didn't mean that my relationship — such as it was at this point — was any less sincere.

"I told you I'm working on that. I bet he's down at the office this very minute tearing through the files." I deepened my voice. " 'That girl — that girl! I've got to find out who she is!' "

"Kobie, the man's probably married. Why bother liking somebody that old?"

"He's not that old," I said defensively. "And he can't be married. We wouldn't have looked at each other that way if he was. You know how boring married people are." I embroidered the dream that had been spinning in my head the last two days.

"Older men are more dependable than boys. T.E. and I will be the perfect couple. We'll go steady, just like you and Doug. He'll give me his college ring — " I especially liked that touch, a college ring was a lot classier than an onyx ring any day. "I'll meet his friends and he'll meet mine. We could even double-date, me and T.E. and you and Doug."

Gretchen snorted. "Double-date with a teacher! Kobie, what's in that gum you're chewing? Your mother won't even let you go to the movies with a boy until you're sixteen, much less date a grown man!"

"So I haven't ironed out all the wrinkles yet. The course of true love never runs smoothly," I quoted. "A little trouble makes it more romantic."

Mrs. Antle patrolled behind our chairs. "Kobie, Gretchen, get busy. I'm going to separate you girls if you can't stop chattering."

"Yes, Mrs. Antle." Obediently Gretchen placed her hands on the keys, her fingernails, painted a pretty shade of pink, curving over the row. I was *so* envious of those fingernails. Her nails had grown long and feminine since she started going with Doug McNeil.

Mrs. Antle also noticed Gretchen's nails. "Cut those claws, Gretchen. A good typist keeps her nails clipped short."

I looked down at my own ragged nails. Love affected people in the strangest ways. It made one girl write in her science book. It made Gretchen's nails grow long, like drinking gelatin every day. But love hadn't seemed to affect me yet.

Of course, I had only fallen in love with T.E. last week. In another week or so, after T.E. and I were going steady, my fingernails would be as long as Gretchen's. Maybe longer.

Chapter 5

His name, Sandy found out from one of his students, was Mr. Brown. Rather dull and disappointing, considering the color of his eyes, but I was sure T.E. had a grand *first* name, like Montgomery or Andrew. He taught freshman shop and was good friends with my algebra teacher, Mr. Bell.

For some strange reason, he didn't notice me after I returned to school. I couldn't understand it, because I knew he must have been as jolted as I was the Day Our Eyes Met. Sandy thought maybe he was more like shell-shocked, afraid to let his feelings for me show.

"I have a plan," Sandy said one day in October. Ordinarily, to hear her utter those four words would be enough to send me running for cover. "I know how to get T.E. to notice you," she added enticingly.

It was all Gretchen's fault I had to rely

on somebody as unreliable as Sandy Robertson. If Gretchen had been behaving like the best friend she was supposed to be, I wouldn't even have listened to Sandy.

I couldn't talk to Gretchen anymore. Excuse me, not Gretchen, but *Gretchen-and-Doug*. You see, Gretchen was no longer an individual person. She and Doug McNeil were an item around Oakton. They were going steady, which evidently meant exchanging rings, not eating lunch, pledging to be with each other as many hours a day as possible, and ignoring best friends and the rest of the world in general.

To be truthful, Gretchen-and-Doug made me more than a little sick. You never saw one without the other attached at the hand, hip, or lip. They floated down the halls, lost in their private fog, either holding hands, or with their arms wound around each other's waists, or kissing. Kissing on school grounds was strictly forbidden, one of those rules that was impossible to enforce, like not cutting in line.

Gretchen-and-Doug even lingered by her locker, which Doug now used so forty seconds of togetherness wouldn't be wasted while he got his books out of his own locker, heads nearly touching, murmuring what appeared to be endearments. I boldly eavesdropped once and heard Gretchen coo to Doug, "Do you have that test in geometry today?" to which Doug softly replied, "Yeah, but I forgot to study."

Doug materialized outside Gretchen's classes like smoke from a genie's lamp, whether the class let out early or late, to escort her to her next one. He carried her books hooked under his right arm in order to hold her hand.

Hand-holding was a position that could not be broken, like a sorcerer's spell. One time I met Gretchen-and-Doug in the corridor between the gym and science wings. A janitor's mop and bucket barricaded one side of the hall, leaving the narrowest of passageways. Gretchen-and-Doug were joined at the wrist that day and, even though it was obvious that I could not get by unless they split up or I polevaulted over them, the three of us danced and dodged the bucket until I managed to slither past.

"You *do* come unlinked, don't you?" I asked, hanging my foot in the wet strands of the soapy mop. "What do you do when it's time to go home?" I pictured Gretchen-and-Doug disentangling at the bus stop every afternoon, parting with a *pop* sound, like a suction cup pried from a tile wall.

Sickening. Yet the sight of them made me feverish with jealousy. I yearned to be one of those hyphenated couples, to be paired off with a boy. But not just any boy. I longed to be the other half of Kobie-and-T.E., if he'd ever notice me.

I tried to talk to Gretchen about my problem on the bus, one of the rare occasions that Gretchen was Doug-less, only because Doug McNeil lived in another section of the school district. I wondered why Gretchen-and-Doug didn't fix that by making the superintendent rezone the boundaries in order to be on the same bus route, or beg their parents to move so they could live next door to each other.

But even when I was alone with Gretchen, she wasn't really there. "Gretch," I said. "I have to talk to you about T.E. It isn't working out quite like I thought. He doesn't seem to know I'm alive."

"Mmmmm." Gretchen was dreamily writing *Mrs. Douglas McNeil* just beneath *Gretchen Farris McNeil* on a scrap of typing paper.

"Gretch, did you hear me? I need some advice."

"About what?"

"About *T.E.*" Honestly, she was deaf as a stone these days.

"I don't know," she finally replied. "I have to ask Doug and see what he thinks."

"I don't want Doug to know I'm in love with a teacher!" I yelled, practically spilling my secret to everybody on the bus. "What do *you* think?"

"I have to ask Doug."

Was it any wonder I turned to Sandy Robertson?

"I should *follow* him?" I repeated, when Sandy unveiled her latest harebrained scheme. "Where?"

"Everywhere," Sandy said. "Whenever you see him in the hall, follow him. But don't walk behind him. Sort of walk beside him, so he'll see you."

"I don't know." I sounded as vague as Gretchen. "He might not like it."

As she spoke, the object of my desire sauntered down the hall, innocently heading toward the industrial arts wing. He looked taller today, his turquoise eyes brightly offset by his yellow shirt. My heart swelled like a puffy satin Valentine. How I loved him!

"There he goes," I said, tracking his progress down the hall.

"He *is* cute," Sandy agreed. "I was thinking about falling in love with a teacher myself, just like you did, but you've already picked the cutest teacher in the school."

T.E. passed without even a glance in my direction. "He never even saw me," I said forlornly.

"He will." Sandy stuck her pencil behind one ear, suddenly businesslike. If I had been operating on all cylinders, I would have sensed the reversal in our roles at that moment. Sandy was about to take control of my life — at least the romance part of it — and I, too lovesick to realize what was happening, let her.

Thus I began a dual life. There was the outwardly normal Kobie Roberts who wore heather-toned skirts and matching sweaters and worried over math and archery practice like any other sophomore girl. Then there was the *other* Kobie Roberts, the one who slinked around Oakton, following the unsuspecting Mr. Brown, alias T.E.

When T.E. failed to notice the small, pointy-faced eager-eyed girl jouncing alongside of him as he strode to the teacher's lounge or to the cafeteria, Sandy increased her intelligence-gathering tactics.

"After third, he usually goes out to his car to get a thermos," she reported, consulting the clipboard on which she plotted T.E.'s every move in minute detail. "Walk out with him and say something like, 'Isn't it a nice day?'"

"'Isn't it a nice day!'" I scoffed. "It's pouring for the twenty-seventh day in a row. Sandy, T.E. *knows* I'm there, but he's deliberately ignoring me."

"That's because he's afraid of his feelings. What you want to do is get him to look at you like he did that day outside math class. Get in front of him. Bump into him accidentally-on-purpose. Make him see you."

"But he never *does*. I might as well go around with a bag over my head." To emphasize my point, I pulled my sweater up over my shoulders, wrapped it around my head, covering my face, and tied the sleeves in a tight knot under my chin. "You think he'd notice me any better like this?" I asked, my voice muffled through the cloth.

"The plan will work. Stick with it," Sandy urged. "Don't let up for a single minute."

Just then she clutched my arm in a death grip. "Here he comes! Now's your chance, Kobie!"

"My chance to do *what*?" I couldn't see with the stupid sweater over my face. "Get me out of this thing!" I pawed frantically at the knot, but it held fast.

"No time!" Sandy shoved me sideways, the sweater still snugly turbaned around my head.

"Not like this!" But it was too late. I was already moving, a prime example of that famous law of physics: an object in motion tends to remain in motion until she has made a complete fool of herself. Spinning across the hall, I ricocheted off the lockers, then bumbled back again, blindly grabbing at other people's coats and jackets.

"Sandy, where are you?" I cried.

Laughter echoed up and down the hall. "Boy, somebody sure pulled the wool over her eyes," some kid quipped, and the others groaned at his terrible joke.

"Will somebody *help* me?" I demanded, before tripping over a rather large shoe.

Two strong hands gripped me above the elbows and lifted me to my feet.

"Young lady," said an amused voice, "you ought to watch where you're going." He steered me out of the stream of traffic and stood me up against the wall, the way you would position a dummy in a department store window.

"Need some help getting that off?" he asked.

"No, thanks," I replied nonchalantly through the left sleeve, as if having a sweater tied over my head was an everyday occurrence. "I'm fine. Really."

"Well, if you're sure — "

"You'd better hurry or you'll miss your class," I insisted.

The amusement level in his voice heightened. "I certainly don't want to do that."

He must have left because the next thing I heard was Sandy's voice chirping, "Kobie, are you okay? Are you okay?"

"Sandy, I'm the laughingstock of Oakton and I'm suffocating in this sweater, but other than that, I couldn't be better. There's one teensy little thing, though."

"What's that?"

"Get me out of this sweater so I can kill you!"

She ripped the sweater off me the hard way, naturally, jamming the buttons up my nose and nearly severing an ear in the process.

"Tell me that the nice man who brought me over here was not T.E. Tell me I did not make an idiot of myself in front of the very man I want to impress so he'll love me back. Tell me that didn't happen, Sandy Robertson."

Sandy wasn't even contrite. She flashed me that green-eyed grin. "At least he noticed you."

"But he didn't know who I was! With my head covered up, he couldn't tell me apart from any other dumb girl in this school, though I ought to be thankful for that."

She pursed her lips. "You wanted T.E. to notice you, and when he does, you get mad at me. There's just no satisfying some people."

A day distinguished by blundering into my true love with a sweater over my head couldn't possibly get worse. But that was before Stuart Buckley nailed me in French class.

"Hey, Kobie, you're a girl — " Stuart shouted as soon as I walked in the door.

I sat down, feeling at least a hundred and twelve. Sandy's schemes were aging me prematurely. "Really, Stuart. You shouldn't be so generous with compliments."

"No, wait." For once, he seemed genuinely upset. "You have to help me."

"With what?"

"It's about — I need to know what girls think of me," he stammered.

My heart hardened. "What *girls* think of you or what *one* girl in particular thinks of you." I had a sneaky suspicion where this discussion was leading.

"One girl . . . two girls . . ." He wiggled his fingers. "What's the difference? Since you're a girl — "

"We've already established that fact."

" — you should know all about these things."

"*What* things?" Why did he talk in riddles all of a sudden?

"About what girls like in boys." He leaned so far into the aisle, he nearly fell out of his desk. "Take Rosemary Swan, for instance — "

I groaned. "Are you still crazy about her?"

"Would she go for a guy like me, you know, who's a little shorter than her, do you think?"

"A little shorter! You're at least a foot — " I stopped when I saw the earnest, pinched look on his face. He really wanted to know if I thought his height, or lack of it, would be an obstacle in dating Rosemary. I decided to break it to him gently. "Stuart, why don't you set your sights a little lower? I'm sure there are lots of shorter girls in this school, just as pretty as Rosemary and maybe a whole lot nicer, who'd be dying to go out with you."

His upper lip stiffened and I realized I had injured his finer side, though to be truthful, I didn't know Stuart even *had* a finer side.

"You're just jealous," he said bitterly. "You'd probably like to have me all to yourself, wouldn't you, Kobie?"

"Jealous! Me? Well, that's gratitude." Where did that little shrimp get off thinking I was losing sleep over *him*. "Why did you ask my advice if you weren't going to take it?"

"Because I thought you'd tell me something better than that," he said, huffily opening his French book, a gesture that spoke of his contempt for me, since Stuart never studied. "I should have known you'd let me down."

He refused to speak to me the rest of the period.

The next day Stuart stalked into class late, confidently stumping past Rosemary Swan's desk. He was definitely taller, but he hadn't *grown* any, certainly not overnight.

When he sat down at his own desk, he tossed me a smirk of triumph. Rosemary Swan had noticed him, all right.

"What did you do?" I asked him. "Sleep on a rack?"

"It's my shoes," Stuart replied. "I put blocks of wood in them. Pretty neat, eh? Did you see her face when I walked by?"

Wood blocks in his shoes yet! The lengths we went to to be noticed by the ones we loved.

Chapter 6

Just as Dr. Wampler predicted, I caught a cold in November that developed into tonsillitis. I stayed home one day, taking medicine until my temperature dropped, and then it was back to the old grind.

"My throat hurts," I complained to my mother as she heartlessly packed me a little "survival" sack containing my pills, lemon throat lozenges, and a pack of tissues.

"I know," she said. "But it'll be better in a few days. As long as you don't have a temperature, you can go to school."

"But I feel awful! It hurts to swallow and I ache all over."

"Kobie, you're going to have to put up with it. You can't miss a week of school every time you get tonsillitis. You're in high school now and your grades are important. If you feel worse, call me and I'll come get you."

I shuffled despondently to the front door. "You'd send me to school in an iron lung. A person has to produce a death certificate in this house to stay home. You don't love me."

"Don't push me, not after yesterday." She hugged me. "Stop dramatizing. You're not dying."

Not that she'd care if I was. Still, I had her promise. If I dragged myself off to school the next day with no argument, she'd let me have Gretchen and Sandy over to spend the night.

"Night-spending!" she exclaimed yesterday, as if I had requested something outrageous. "That's all you kids think about, spending the night at somebody else's house."

" *'Night-spending?'* " I repeated. "Mother, must you sound so nineteenth century? It's a *slumber* party."

"When I was growing up," she began in that mother tone that brought to mind hoop skirts and buggy whips and one-room schoolhouses, "I never thought of spending the night at my friend's house. In my day, you went to sleep in your own bed."

"In your day, you slept in the same room with two of your sisters. In the same bed with Aunt Lil. You had a slumber party every night."

"Some party," she said scornfully. "Lil kicking me and hogging the covers."

Now, as I shrugged into my stadium coat, I reminded her of the promise. "I'm asking Gretchen and Sandy if they can come *this weekend*."

"Only if you're better."

"If I'm well enough to go to school, I'm well enough to have my friends over Saturday. Aren't I?" I asked.

Mother handed me my muffler with a sharp glance. "You're getting too smart, Kobie." But she said it in such a way I knew I had won.

Some victory. I really and truly felt yucky. Because I had the chills, I kept my muffler wound around my neck, even in gym. The scarf was striped burgundy and gold, the school colors the committee finally settled on, and I figured people would think I was displaying school spirit by wearing the colors all the time. Unfortunately, a long striped muffler did not go well with my gym suit or any of my outfits. Instead of hiding my condition, I attracted unwanted stares and comments. Once again I had my old Woodson reputation, the one I had tried so hard to bury. People thought I was weird.

Except for Gretchen, no one knew my sordid secret. Even letting people think I was weird was a notch better than letting them know I had tonsillitis, a sickness only little kids got.

"You just dipped your scarf in your gravy," Eddie Showalter said at lunch later that week.

"Thanks." I wiped gravy from the tasseled ends of my muffler. The thing was really a nuisance, forever falling in my food and getting caught on the handle of my locker.

"Are you cold?"

"Of course not. What makes you think I'm cold?" I fanned my napkin furiously, pretending to be hot to erase his impression that there might be something wrong with me. "I wish they'd turn the heat down in this cafeteria. I'm burning up."

"It *is* a little stuffy in here," he agreed amiably.

Eddie Showalter had camped at my lunch table ever since the note-amnesia episode. Like a puppy dumped on a doorstep, Eddie just sort of stayed. Sandy conveniently disappeared during lunch about four days out of five, leaving me and Eddie alone.

Eddie was usually at our table when I sat down with my tray, his science book or Spanish book in front of him. He never turned the page and he never ate.

He was pleasant to be around. He never bugged me like Stuart did, instead asking how my drawing was coming along, and sometimes showing me his own sketches, chiefly of the White House and jet airplanes. His ninth-grade obsession to be both a pilot *and* president had not cooled.

"The only way you'll get in the White House," I told him, examining a tiny crosshatched view of the East Wing, "is with a ticket like the rest of us."

"Anyone can aspire to the top office," Eddie said. "Everyone has the same chance in this country."

"I think you've been watching too many corn flakes commercials."

He changed the subject. "Are you going to the game?" Our school was playing Marshall High. "They might bring the real mascot."

In addition to choosing burgundy and gold as the school colors, we voted to have a cougar as mascot. A local farmer who had raised a pair of cougars from cubs offered to lend our school one of the cats, chained and caged, for halftime at big games. A goat would fill in for the rest of the games.

"After watching our team at the pep rally last Friday, they might as well bring the goat," I said.

Oakton had only a junior varsity team and a pretty pathetic one at that. Witnessing our pitiful team stumble out onto the field to the manic cheers of our equally stumbling cheerleaders and the off-key music of our band did little to instill hope we would beat Marshall, or even Oakton Elementary in a game of kickball.

"I'm probably going," Eddie said, suddenly glancing down at his science book. His eyelashes were long, longer than mine no matter how many coats of mascara I put on. "I thought I might see you there."

My throat tightened, a reaction that had nothing to do with tonsillitis. Was Eddie asking me, in a roundabout way, if I'd go to the game with him? "Well, actually, I'm busy Friday."

"Oh. You're going out, then."

"Not exactly." Why didn't I tell him Sandy and Gretchen were coming over? Why lead him to believe I had a date, an event as unlikely as striking oil in my backyard.

"I should have guessed you'd be busy," Eddie said. "You're probably booked up weeks ahead."

"Months," I said airily, although anybody who spent more than three minutes in my company knew my social calendar was free until the end of the century.

Stuart would have guffawed over the notion that I was popular enough to actually be busy on a Friday night, but Eddie accepted my greatly exaggerated status as one of the "right" people.

Sandy leaped at my invitation to a mini-slumber party, but Gretchen was a lot tougher to persuade. She couldn't bear to be away from Doug on one of their regular date nights, she said. You could always call him, I argued. It wasn't the same thing, she said. At last I convinced her it was entirely possible for her to have a good time at my house even *without* Doug. When she relented, I felt exhausted.

Friday night the three of us went to see *Romeo and Juliet*. By the time we got back from the movies, my mother had set up a camp cot and an old chaise lounge in my room. There wasn't an inch of space to walk in, but that didn't matter since all we did was loll first in one bed and then the other, playing records, leafing through magazines, and listening to Gretchen sigh.

Gretchen was turning into a real party-pooper. She drooped around like a moulting chicken.

"Stop mourning," I told her. "Doug didn't go off to war."

"I know. But I *miss* him." And she let loose another gusty sigh, like the wind caught high in the treetops. Most annoying.

By eleven-thirty we had annihilated a bacon pizza, three packs of Ho-Ho's, five RCs, a bowl of Fritos, a pan of brownies, plus all that junk at the movies, and we were wondering when my mother was going to bring us some *real* food when

Sandy suddenly cried, "Here's your answer, Kobie! Here's how to get T.E. to notice you!"

"What is it?" I struggled over to my bed where Sandy was stretched out reading Gretchen's *Seventeen*.

"Right here." Sandy held up the glossy advertisement so I could see it. "Just like in the movie. It's perfect for you, Kobie."

In the ad, a beautiful girl modeled an updated Juliet gown with deep lace sleeves dripping over her wrists, to illustrate the girl's pearly pink nails. *The romantic look is always in,* the ad proclaimed, praising a brand of lipstick and nail polish.

"You buy this stuff," Sandy said, "and you get a soft pretty dress and T.E. will fall for you just like Romeo fell for Juliet."

"I'd look awful in an Empire-waist dress," I said. "I haven't got any bust as it is — that style will make me look even flatter."

Sandy scrutinized my figure, which of course did not show to advantage in the rumpled pajamas I was wearing. "Well, maybe not a dress exactly like this one. But something pretty. You're good at drawing. Why don't you draw your own?"

"You mean, design my own dress?"

"Yeah. And maybe fix your hair different. That girl's hair isn't any longer than yours — you could curl it and put a ribbon in it. And stop carrying your books on your hip."

"How do you want me to carry them? On my head? What does that have to do with looking romantic for T.E.?"

"Hold your books like this." She cradled the magazine to her chest. "*You* carry them on your hip, like the boys do."

I actually considered her suggestions, demonstrating the depths of my hopelessness over T.E. Heeding beauty tips offered by Sandy Robertson was like asking Dracula where he went to the dentist.

One day last summer, Sandy, Gretchen, and I all bought the same makeup and practiced putting it on. Gretchen was a natural and could sub as an Avon Lady. Because I could draw well, my hand was the steadiest with the eyeliner brush. But Sandy! Her blush-on was like tire treads, her mascara tipped her lashes in little globules, and her eyeliner was thick and crooked.

Even with these facts uppermost in my mind, I heard myself say, "So you really think the romantic look will attract T.E.? You know, if I didn't tape my hair, it would be curly like that model's." I minced around the camp cot. "Am I walking like Rosemary Swan?"

"Swing to the right. That's it," Sandy coached. "Don't you think Kobie will make a great Juliet?" she asked Gretchen.

Gretchen, who was moping over not being able to call Doug any more that night, sighed so hard she nearly blew the sheets off the beds.

"She left with no forwarding address," I said to Sandy. "Anyway, she doesn't believe I should waste my time over a teacher. Do you, Gretchen?" I yelled in her face.

"No," she replied absentmindedly. Then, injecting a little strength into her voice, "Kobie, this whole business with the shop teacher is stupid. The man is probably married."

"He doesn't wear a ring," Sandy put in.

"That doesn't prove anything. Neither does my father. He's allergic to gold," Gretchen said.

Sandy asked thoughtfully, "Why doesn't he wear a silver ring?"

Gretchen threw her a dark look. "Will you grow up? The point is that Kobie is going to make a fool of herself over this teacher and for what? She's only fifteen. Her mother isn't going to let her date a man that old — "

"Shhhhhh! Do you want her to *hear?*" I knew if my mother thought I was interested in a teacher, she'd have me in reform school until I was thirty.

"There isn't *that* much difference in their ages," Sandy defended. "My father is older than my mother and he says the age gap closes the older they get."

"Fifteen is too young for a grown man," Gretchen said primly, sounding like our old fourth-grade teacher. "What would he see in a girl like Kobie? To him, she's just a kid."

"I am not! According to my doctor, I'm an adult. We're all adults in this room. Mostly," I added with a glance at Sandy.

The remark sailed right over Sandy's head. "We start driver's ed next week. Pretty soon we'll get our licenses."

"*Classroom* driver's ed," Gretchen corrected. "We won't be allowed to get behind the wheel until next summer."

I didn't expect to get behind the wheel until I was old enough to buy my own car. My mother had only learned to drive the year before, sufficiently frightening my father, who decreed he would never teach anyone to drive ever again. Gretchen would get her learner's permit before me, naturally, and she'd zoom off into the sunset with Doug, leaving me stranded and dateless.

Our party mood hit a snag. Gretchen resumed her sighing and pining. Sandy wondered when my mother was going to bring fresh rations. I sat on the chaise lounge and imagined the beautiful dress I would design, the one that would make T.E. fall to his knees when he saw me.

Chapter 7

Saturday evening I decided to get my homework out of the way. Algebra problems, an English paper, French, the usual stuff. But inside my physical science notebook was a reminder: *bring slug to school.*

I had forgotten all about that stupid assignment! The last thing Mr. Chapman had called out as the bell rang was for each of us to bring a *slug* to class for some weird biology experiment. I couldn't imagine a lesson involving thirty-five slugs.

My parents were having a snack at the kitchen table and discussing the necessity of having our septic tank pumped in the spring, a topic that went nicely with coffee and oatmeal cookies, when I interrupted.

"Where are your old boots?" I asked my father. "I have to go out in the garden and look for a slug for school."

"You can't go out in the damp and look for slugs until you're over your sore throat," my mother said, never turning a hair at the silliness of such an assignment. My mother seldom questioned anything I did for school; she firmly believed my teachers knew what they were doing.

"It rains every day. I can't wait until it stops," I protested, more to be argumentative than anything. I wasn't really that enthusiastic about hunting for a slug.

My father finished his cookie in one bite. "Never saw such a wet fall. If it snows as much as it's rained, we'll be snowbound till July." He drank the rest of his coffee. "I'll get you a slug, Kobie."

"I need it for Monday," I said, relieved. Digging through a bunch of dead wet leaves for an icky, slimy slug was hardly something I was eager to do. My father wouldn't have much luck finding one either, since slugs probably inched south for the winter. I looked up slugs in my encyclopedia, in case Mr. Chapman popped a quiz, and learned they are actually pulmonate gastropods. I had gone fifteen years thinking they were just snails too poor to afford a little house to carry around on their backs.

The next day I was designing romantic dresses when my father called me from the back porch. I went out to see what he wanted.

Holding a five-gallon bucket by the handle, he grinned proudly. "I bet none of the other kids will have beauties like these." He tipped the bucket forward so I could see inside.

If I hadn't been raised in the country, I probably would have fainted at the sight of the two huge leopard-spotted slugs wiggling on the bed of moss at the bottom of the bucket. At the very least I would have screamed.

Instead I asked, "Where did you get such big ones? Not out of our garden?" If he had, I wasn't setting foot off the porch as long as I lived here.

"In the woods," he replied, and I saw his pants were soaked to the knees. "Under a rotted log. You have to know where to look. What'll your teacher think when you show him?"

My heart fell somewhere around my heels as I realized I would have to take those huge prehistoric slugs to *school.* Despair was followed by a rash of guilt. Once before I complained to my mother about the way my father always went around in his green school-board uniform. "So he doesn't get dressed up in a suit," my mother had snapped at me. "He works hard to earn us a decent living. You should be ashamed, making fun of him."

Even without my mother to accuse me, I felt ashamed again. Here my father had slogged through the rainy woods and lifted countless logs to get me the biggest and best slugs any kid ever took to school, and I didn't want them. I wanted ordinary garden-variety slugs that wouldn't cause people to stampede.

"Maybe my teacher will be scared of them," I said hopefully. "I wouldn't want to give Mr. Chapman a heart attack. He's only expecting us to bring in little bitty slugs." Certainly not Godzilla and his brother.

"Those little bitty things the other kids'll have will look sick next to these fine specimens," my father said. Actually, I thought it might be the other way around.

"I only have a small glass jar," I said, grasping at any excuse now. "They won't fit in it."

"We'll fix up something," my father reassured me. "Don't worry."

Monday morning, I let my hair curl naturally, put on a pale pink blouse with a lace collar, and was all set to conquer T.E. with my new romantic look when my mother handed me an enormous Tupperware box along with my lunch money.

"Don't forget your science project," she said.

Gingerly I piled the box on top of my books. "This looks like a bread box."

"It is." She pried open one corner of the

hole-punched lid. "Your father put wet moss inside, so the slugs will rest comfortably." She closed the lid quickly. "Awful-looking, aren't they? You ought to get an A."

Like my father, my mother thought size was related to good marks. "Mom, I can't take these horrible things to school! I'm wearing a pink blouse!"

"What does that have to do with your project?"

Nothing I could make her understand without revealing my campaign. "Tupperware clashes with pink," I said weakly.

Her patience suddenly frayed, like an old rope. "You take this box to school and stop acting like such a brat, Kobie Roberts. Your father tramped half the day Sunday, his only day off, to find you those slugs. You should be grateful."

"I am! I'm grateful to be carrying the biggest, grossest slugs in the history of the world to school on the day when I want to look pretty! I'm also late." I pulled on my coat and left without kissing my mother good-bye. I didn't know what had gotten into her. Instead of our fighting occasionally, say, once a day, it was just one long fight with her lately.

Gretchen was writing Doug a note when I sat down beside her on the bus.

"Good grief," I exclaimed, glimpsing the

mushy greeting. "You're going to see him in about forty minutes."

"I know, but this is for him to read in first period. Then he'll answer me back and I'll read it in second period and so on. That way we can talk to each other all day."

"Honestly, Gretchen, why don't you two just elope?"

She looked up from her tablet. "What's eating you?"

"You are! You haven't said one word about my hair. Why go to all the trouble of wearing it different if nobody's going to notice?" I shifted the books in my lap, jiggling the Tupperware box.

"You hair looks very nice," Gretchen said dutifully. "What's in the box?"

"Our science assignment. Remember? Mr. Chapman asked us to bring in a slug. Where's yours?" I didn't see any evidence of a jar or box.

"I think Doug is bringing one for each of us."

"You mean you don't absolutely know for sure what Doug McNeil is doing this second? Did your walkie-talkies break down? No, wait — I've got it. He's going to surprise you with a slug set in gold and onyx so you can wear it around your neck."

"Boy, somebody got up on the wrong side of the bed."

"You'd be grouchy, too, if you had to lug around this stupid bread box." I tapped the lid angrily.

"Why didn't you use something smaller?" For the first time in ages, Gretchen's curiosity was roused. "What *have* you got in there? Let me see."

"You don't really want to do that." I didn't want to be blamed for her heart attack.

"Oh, come on," she pleaded. "Just let me peek."

"All right, you asked for it." I yanked the lid off, exposing my pulmonate gastropods in all their slimy leopard-spotted splendor.

"AAAAAAAACK!" Gretchen reeled backward, scattering books and papers and Doug's letter in a panicky wake. "Kobie, you — you! Why didn't you *warn* me?"

"I tried."

"You're perfectly horrid, Kobie Roberts! I'm not sitting with you!" She flew down the aisle to find another seat.

Guilt engulfed me for the second time in two days. It *was* mean to spring those dinosaurs on Gretchen like that. I guess I was tired of her smugness over Doug, as if she were rubbing my face in the fact that she had a boyfriend and I didn't.

You wouldn't think an entire school

would go ape over a couple of meatloaf-sized slugs in a Tupperware bread box, but that's what happened. Rumor that I had two slugs with glandular problems spread like a brush fire, and before I knew it, every guy in the tenth grade crowded around me to see what I had in the box. I couldn't have been more popular if I had given away tickets to the Superbowl. Or more embarrassed.

If I hadn't been such a tenderhearted person, I would have chucked those monsters in the nearest trash can. But I felt responsible for them; after all, they had been minding their own business when my father ripped them from their happy home under the rotten log. My conscience wouldn't let me leave the box in my locker, so I was stuck with the blob twins until fourth period.

Mr. Chapman greeted me with a smile. "I've been hearing about your prize gastropods all day." As he lifted the lid, he turned an interesting shade of green but bravely put his hand inside and brought out Godzilla I and II.

"Do you think your father could get me three or four?" Sandy asked as we raced to math in the industrial arts wing. "They're great for attracting boys."

"Did you check your IQ at the door?

How would you like to go around all day with slug juice on your sleeve?" The girl's elevator clearly did not go to the top.

Sandy stepped on my foot, crushing my big toe in her haste to back up. "Look, there's T.E.! Too bad you don't have your little friends with you."

I shoved her off my bruised foot. "Wouldn't that have been romantic? I'm glad he didn't see me before now. It was awful enough I had to run into him with a sweater over my head." I patted my hair, making sure it was still curly. "At least now he knows I have pretty hair."

T.E. didn't look up until he was in front of me. His beautiful turquoise eyes met mine in startled recognition. Then he whirled around as if he suddenly remembered a previous appointment and hurried in the other direction.

"Why did he turn and run?" I cried, dismayed. "Do I look that bad?"

T.E. didn't act the slightest bit gallant and suave, the way he'd been the day he'd helped me across the traffic-clogged hall. Was he only nice to girls with sweaters over their heads? Or had he heard about my mega-gastropods and was afraid I'd sic them on him?

I sniffed my armpit. "I bet my deodorant failed. Sandy, he hates me!"

"No, he doesn't. He *likes* you. Can't you

see — he's afraid to let you know how much he likes you."

Of course. It made perfect sense. In novels men were forever denying their feelings for the women they loved.

"I told you this new plan would work," she said. "Romance gets 'em every time."

"Not quite. How do I get him to run in *my* direction, not the other way?" What would I have to do to attract him? Send up flares?

"The dress," Sandy stated. "You need a beautiful dress, like Juliet's."

Designing a romantic dress wasn't that easy. It required intense concentration, lots of paper, plenty of Twinkies, and the right mood. In order to put myself into a romantic mood, I played my new album over and over, a lot of love-gone-wrong songs that my mother said sounded like funeral dirges.

"Kobie," she barked from the hall. "If you play that ghastly record one more time, I'm leaving home!"

"There's nothing wrong with this record," I yelled back. "Plug your ears if you don't like it."

"Why don't you play *real* music? Anything would be better than that awful racket. I'd rather listen to . . . Elvis Presley!" she concluded in desperation.

"*El*-vis *Pres*-ley! Mom, you are so out of it." I selected a gray felt-tip pen to color in the chinchilla cuffs of the Russian-style coatdress I had created.

My mother hung around my door. "I may be out of it, but at least I know good music when I hear it."

"Mother, I like this record and I'm going to keep playing it."

"You might come home and find a big scratch across it," she said menacingly.

"Then I'll buy another one."

"What do those songs *mean*? About the jewels and binoculars on moose antlers. What's that supposed to mean?"

I wouldn't get any peace by ignoring her. "It doesn't mean *anything*. It just *is*. I don't try to analyze it — I just listen to the words and let the pictures flow through my mind."

"But the pictures are all *weird*."

"I know. That's why I like it."

She went away then, shaking her head over the decline of my generation and how she dreaded placing her future in the hands of people who grew up listening to such drivel.

I colored my Russian coatdress with the silver felt-tip pen, thinking of the futility of parents and teenagers trying to communicate.

Chapter 8

"What's that?" Stuart asked, reaching for a paper poking out of my notebook.

We were in French, writing an essay about these mountain climbers lost in the Alps. At least, *I* was writing; Stuart was angling to copy off mine.

I swatted his grubby little fingers. "Hands off."

"Why can't I see? It's one of those Mickey Mouse pictures, isn't it? How come you never show me your drawings? You let everybody else see them but not me. You don't like me anymore."

Now I understood the principle of the Chinese water torture — just keep at somebody, drop by drop, until she caves in.

The drawing Stuart tried to steal from my notebook was not one of my Disney cartoons, but the dress I had designed, the one that would topple T.E. I didn't want Stuart to see it. I didn't want anyone to see it, not Stuart or Sandy or even Gretchen.

Designing this dress had been an almost mystical experience. For weeks, I had crumpled up dozens of designs that were either too impractical to make, like the Persian lamb and chinchilla coatdress, or just didn't do anything for my particular figure type (Classic Bed Slat). But yesterday my pen started sketching with a life of its own, and suddenly, there it was. *The* dress.

Tiers of gathered white lace attached to a white satin underskirt, the lacy ruffles falling from an emerald velvet yoke to just above the knee. Flowing chiffon sleeves cuffed with pearl buttons, a green velvet bow tied at the neckline, the ends of the ribbon drifting over the wedding-cake lace. Juliet would have sold her Capulet name for a dress like this.

The dress was so breathtakingly beautiful, I couldn't believe it came out of my head. Half afraid the design would evaporate, I brought it to school and checked every so often to make sure the paper hadn't gone blank. Every time I saw the sketch, I felt all trembly inside — that dress was going to change my life. I wasn't ready to share my creation with the world. Not yet.

But Stuart was still badgering me. "You never let me see your dumb old drawings. What kind of a friend are you?"

"Stuart, the last time I showed you my drawings, you made fun of them."

"That was years ago. We were little kids then."

It was only *two* years ago and one of us still qualified as little. Fortunately, I could shut him up because I also had with me one of the preliminary sketches from the *Lady and the Tramp* series I was working on before fashion design consumed my spare time.

"Here," I said, flinging a torn piece of sketch paper at him. "No smart remarks."

The drawing was from the scene in the movie where Tramp and Lady share a romantic spaghetti dinner behind an Italian restaurant. The two dogs are eating the same strand of spaghetti, not knowing that they are going to wind up in a kiss. The expression of sweet canine innocence in their eyes, especially in Lady's, was difficult to achieve and I wasn't sure I had it. I brought the drawing with me to get a new perspective.

"This is great! You really are a terrific artist! Such talent," Stuart gushed. If I'd been wearing false teeth, I would have dropped them on the floor.

"What do you want?" I asked, instantly

alert. "If you're buttering me up to let you copy my essay, forget it — "

"I don't want anything," he said, astonished that such an outlandish thought had crossed my mind. "Except maybe this."

"My drawing? You want my picture? What on earth for?"

"Gretchen has a whole bunch of your pictures. Why not me?" he said. "I'd really like to own a Kobie Roberts original. Some day when you're famous I can say I knew you when."

"When you were driving me crazy, you mean." Yet I was flattered by his request. Could it be that Stuart was interested in me? No, the idea was too unbelievable. Playing the part of the terrific and terribly talented artist, I said, "It's yours. Let me have it back and I'll sign it."

"No, no." Stuart hung onto the drawing. "It'll be worth more this way. If you sign it, it'll be like you knew you were going to be famous and that kind of ruins it. People expect artists to starve and struggle for years and give away their work for nothing."

"Is that so? Now that you've got my future all mapped out, what are *you* going to be doing while I'm starving and struggling?" In the two years I had known Stuart he'd never indicated what he wanted to do beyond squirming out of as much work as he possibly could and still remain in school. Amazingly, he made fairly decent grades.

"I have no idea," he replied.

"What about acting?" I remembered how good he had been as the Artful Dodger in our eighth-grade production of *Oliver!*

"Nah. I don't know what I want to do. I guess I just want to live and have a great time." His sharp gray eyes zeroed in on Rosemary Swan. "And get that girl," he added, almost to himself.

"Good luck."

Stuart had stopped wearing blocks in his shoes to appear taller — the rough chunks of wood gave him blisters, he said. I wondered what course of action he planned to take next to win Rosemary. Too bad he didn't have a scheme as foolproof as mine.

My mother stared at the sketch, then the materials I had listed in one corner.

"You want me to make you this dress," she said finally. "without a pattern, without measurements, without anything to go by except this picture you drew."

I hopped up and down on one foot. "Mom, it's not as hard as it looks. I'll help you."

"Some help you'll be. If you recall, you ruined your sewing project in eighth-grade home ec and *I* had to fix it. Not to mention failing home ec last year." She was never going to let that rest — it would probably be inscribed on my tombstone: *She failed home ec and broke her mother's heart.*

"Mom, I *have* to have this dress. I'll just *die* if I don't have this dress."

"Where are you going that's so important you have to have such a fancy dress?" she demanded.

I couldn't tell her the truth, that I intended to wear the dress to wring an admission of love from T.E. If she knew *that*, she'd lock me in my room and throw the key down the well.

"I — it's for a party," I improvised. "Gretchen's having a big New Year's Eve party and I want to wear it then."

"Clare hasn't said anything about a party." My mother and Gretchen's mother were good friends and frequently exchanged spy reports about me and Gretchen.

"She doesn't know about it yet," I said. "Gretchen and her boyfriend want to get every detail just right before they ask her."

My mother laid my sketch down, momentarily distracted. "That girl is entirely too young to be going steady. I don't believe in dating too soon. There's plenty of time for boys."

When? I'd been fifteen for six whole months — soon I'd be over the hill. But I had to get her back on the subject at hand.

"Mom, I really really need this dress. Can you make it for me?"

She regarded me with that fierce, steely look geared to get a daughter to confess she spilled the nail polish on the tablecloth and ate the dessert meant for company. "Why do you need this dress so badly? Why *this* dress? Why not buy a pretty dress?"

How could I explain that *this* dress was totally unique, that no one else in the world would have a dress like this, that it would make me *special*. While it was important to have the same clothes as the other girls at school, it was suddenly more important to have a dress that was *different*.

"I just want this dress," I whispered, without attempting to put my hazy desires into words.

Something in my tone must have registered with my mother because she said, "All right. I can't promise you it'll turn out just like your picture, but I'll try. *On one condition.*"

"What?" I asked, afraid she would demand an unreasonable favor in return, like washing the dishes every night or scrubbing the basement floor.

"Promise you won't play that infernal record. My nerves can't take it any more."

"Deal." A few weeks without my album was a small sacrifice.

We went to Manassas that weekend. The

stores were decorated with plastic holly and styrofoam reindeer, reminders that Christmas was bearing down on us. In Sew Forth, my mother purchased heavy bridal satin for the underskirt of my dress, tulle to attach the lace to, emerald velvet for the bodice, and a half a yard of chiffon for the sleeves. The pre-gathered lace was the hardest to find. We found a spool of it in Woolworth's and lavishly bought ten yards. It was horribly expensive, even for Woolworth's, but my mother never said a word as she handed the girl at the cash register a twenty-dollar bill.

After such an extravagant spree, I expected to go home for lunch, probably birdseed and distilled water drained out of the steam iron, but my mother headed for the luncheonette counter.

I love eating in Woolworth's. I twirled on my red leather stool, getting swimmy-headed until my mother smacked my knee.

"How old are you?" she asked.

The reprimand didn't bother me. I had the fabric for my beautiful dress and a willing, if somewhat snippish, seamstress to sew it. The world was rosy.

I read the menu carefully, and said, "I want a hot turkey sandwich and a large Coke."

My mother ordered the grilled cheese special. "I can't believe how much money we spent on material today. I must have been delirious to let you talk me into making that dress."

The waitress brought our drinks, spilling them so the sides of the glasses would be sticky. I unwrapped my straw and took a long pull of my Coke.

"I've got an old pattern of yours I can use for the yoke and the length of the dress. The rest I'll have to do without a pattern. Sewing that lace on the tulle will be the worst part."

"You can do it," I said confidently. "If you could fix that shirtwaist dress I made in eighth grade, you can do anything."

"That was a job and a half," she agreed. "Have you thought about Christmas shopping?"

"I have thirty dollars saved. Enough to buy presents for you, Dad, Gretchen, and Sandy. Charles is supposed to take me and Gretchen to the mall next weekend. That is, if she can unglue herself from Doug McNeil."

Bringing up Gretchen's dating situation was a grave mistake. Mom was off.

"Fifteen is too young to be hanging around one boy all the time," she declared as our food arrived. "In fact, fifteen is too young to even be thinking about boys, much less going steady."

"Too young to be thinking about boys!

Mom, what am I supposed to do, shut off my brain? You can't tell me you weren't interested in boys when you were my age."

She bit into her grilled cheese. "My mother wouldn't put up with such foolishness. She'd have tanned my hide if I so much as looked at a boy before I was eighteen. No boys until then, that was the rule."

"What a stupid rule." I never really knew my grandmother; she passed away long ago. "Mom, you told me last year that *this* year, when I was fifteen, things would be better. In fact, you *promised* me. But if I can't date, I might as well still be fourteen."

"I never said any such thing. I said your life would get *easier* — you wouldn't have to fight so, the way you've been the last couple of years. And you aren't. You're more grown up. You've got nice friends, pretty new clothes, a brand-new school to go to — " My mother felt I should be thrilled over Oakton's modern facilities, unable to realize that *no school* was preferable to *new school*.

Whenever we ate in Woolworth's I always ordered the hot turkey sandwich. Usually I'd pile the mashed potatoes on top of the turkey and sprinkle the whole mess with peas and the little cup of cranberry sauce. Today, however, I cut a tiny sliver of the sandwich with my knife and fork and ate it with dignity, hoping to convince my mother I was an adult now, just like her, only not as stodgy.

"If I'm more grown up," I said, daintily wiping cranberry sauce off my mouth, "I ought to be able to go out with a boy."

"What boy?" she demanded, her eyes drilling into mine. "Have you been chasing after some boy, when your father and I told you you can't date until you're sixteen?"

"I haven't been chasing after any boy," I replied truthfully. T.E. couldn't really be classified as a boy and she didn't say anything about chasing after a *teacher*. "But if one did ask me out, what am I supposed to tell him? I'm sorry, but you'll have to wait a year, until I'm sixteen?"

"If he respects you, he'll wait."

"You don't understand. Boys don't care about respect! They just want to go out and have fun. And so do I! Honestly, Mother, you make it sound like a boy has to come to the house and request my hand in marriage before we can go have a slice of pizza."

She rubbed her forehead, as if she had just gotten a terrific headache. "Kobie, I don't want to argue with you about this anymore. No dating till you're sixteen and that's that. If you bring it up again, I'll move it to seventeen. Eat your lunch. I want to get out of here before the traffic."

I didn't speak to her on the drive home; instead, I stared out the window at the stockyard and the Dairy Queen and the muddy Bull Run river and wondered why my mother and I could find no common ground. Sure, she'd relented and bought me expensive material to make my fancy party dress, but she *refused* to bend when it came to dating. I couldn't make her see how wrong she was. Our relationship was like some kind of a dance. One step forward, two steps backward.

Chapter 9

I threw the last of my cinnamon roll into the wire-enclosed aviary, ignoring the sign forbidding people to feed the birds. The finches flitted down from their perches and skittered over to investigate. Gretchen was still eating her bun, chewing slowly, her eyes focused on the bubbling drink machine at the Orange Bowl, where we had bought our midmorning snacks.

"Where to first?" I asked, prodding her out of her reverie. "Spencer's?"

"I guess. I want to buy Doug something funny and something serious. Spencer's is a good place to get a gag gift."

Gretchen had managed to insert Doug's name in every other sentence, no matter how trivial, since her brother Charles had let us off in front of Tyson's Corner mall. Ecstatic since we had nearly a whole day to shop together, *alone*, I decided not to complain, figuring she was sure to purge Doug from her system. After an hour or thereabouts, her Doug mania should taper off.

I wadded my napkin. "Let's get started then."

The mall was decorated to the hilt, swags of evergreens scalloped the storefronts and clusters of mechanical elves bowed and gyrated in the center of the mall. The whole place smelled like a giant candy cane. Christmas was in the air.

I had thirty dollars to spend on presents for my parents, Sandy, and Gretchen. I planned to buy Gretchen's gift while she was elsewhere, hunting for the perfect present for Doug, which, from all outward signs, would take the whole shopping trip.

In Spencer's, Gretchen debated over a rack of fake Snoopy trophies. "Do you think he'd like this one? 'World's Greatest Golfer'? As a souvenir of our third date?" She put the trophy back on the shelf. "No, he might get the wrong idea. The time we played miniature golf was very special — I shouldn't make light of it."

I tried to be helpful, if only to speed things along. "Gretchen, if you like the trophy, get it. It's cute. Anyway, it was only a *date*, not a state funeral."

"You don't understand," she said, forgetting she had asked my advice. "You're not going steady."

Not yet, but I would be very soon. My mother was nearly finished with my dress. As soon as she sewed the last stitch, I'd be able to dazzle T.E. with my ravishing Juliet-like beauty. The man didn't stand a chance.

I bought Sandy a mirrored makeup case before we left Spencer's. It was green plastic, with a mirror in the lid and compartments to hold her lipgloss and eyeshadow. Sandy would love it.

We went on to Hecht's department store, where Gretchen hovered over a selection of men's sweaters.

"What do you think? This one — " she held up a gray and maroon argyle vest " — or this one?" Her second choice was a navy and white crew neck. "Which one do you think he'd look the best in?"

At this point, I thought Doug McNeil would look just fine in a hand-knit strait jacket with a matching muzzle.

"The gray one," I said, wondering when we'd ever get around to buying *my* presents. "It'll go great with his eyes. The other one would make him look like a referee."

"You're right, Kobie. There's just a hint of blue in the weave, the same shade as his eyes. Have you ever really looked at Doug's eyes? I mean really *looked*. They're an incredible color, a deep gray, like the ocean after a storm."

My stomach heaved, either in rebellion over the yeasty cinnamon bun or Gretchen's poetic description. "I can't say I've really noticed Doug's eyes," I replied, "since they're always fastened on you. All I've seen is the back of his head. By the way, did you know his hair is thinning at the crown? He'll probably be bald by the time he's twenty."

"He will not! Doug has nice, thick hair!" she cried indignantly.

Gretchen did not buy the sweater. Our fun day rapidly went downhill as I traipsed after her from one store to the next, unable to resist making nasty little suggestions. ("How about a hammer, Gretch? He could probably use a new one. Here's a pair of G.I. Joe pajamas. I bet he'd love those.")

"Gretchen, don't you have *other* presents besides Doug's to buy?" I asked in Becker's. "Charles, your parents . . . you know, those people who live in the same house with you. Not to mention best friends."

"Shhhh. You're breaking my concentration," she muttered, sweating with indecision over a display of men's jewelry boxes. "This is very important, what I buy Doug. It's our first Christmas together."

"Do you think he's agonizing over what he's getting you? He'll probably zip into People's Drug Store on Christmas Eve five minutes before they close, sniff a couple of colognes, and buy you a bottle of Wind Song or something." I was positive that Edward the Eighth hadn't spent half as much time deliberating over what engagement ring to give Wallis Simpson and *he* had been about to forfeit an entire kingdom.

After two and a half hours, I discovered that mall-shopping was tough on the feet and that a best friend's quest for the Perfect Gift for her steady was taxing on the nerves.

"I quit," I announced in Hoffritz's Cutlery, right in the middle of a Swiss army knife demonstration. "I'm going to get something to eat. You coming or are you going to stay here and count blades?"

Gretchen reluctantly surrendered a nifty forty-nine-dollar job to the clerk. "I know he'd love the one with the can opener and corkscrew, but I don't have enough money," she said sadly.

Observing Gretchen's crazed behavior, I decided that having a boyfriend wasn't worth the trouble and was glad I didn't have one. But then I noticed the way the store lights illuminated the gold and onyx ring hanging around Gertchen's neck.

Whatever Doug put her through, either real or imagined, she wore his ring and the whole world knew she was loved.

I dragged her away from Hoffritz's before she began foaming at the mouth. "Gretchen, this is crazy. It's almost two o'clock and we haven't even eaten lunch yet. Charles will be back to get us at four and I've only bought one piddly present!"

My pep talk must have hit her like a faceful of snow. "I'll go back to Hecht's and buy Doug the gray sweater," she said, and I foolishly believed her. "And then I'll get the little trophy at Spencer's. Then we can go eat."

But we didn't. The sweater still wasn't *quite* what she was looking for. She was certain the perfect present lurked around there *some*place.

What happened next I attribute to the temporary leave of senses one has when deprived of food too long. We staggered past Piercing Pagoda, a little stall in the middle of the fashion court where you can get your ears pierced or just buy earrings. Residue from the sweet roll I had eaten hours ago sent a sugar rush to my brain, causing me to lose control.

I said, "I'm going to get my ears pierced!" Now normally I don't make such hasty decisions, but three hours of watching Gretchen waver over one rotten present had turned me into a rash person.

"Get your ears pierced?" Gretchen repeated. "Do you think you should? Your mother will be furious." Last year when Gretchen had her ears pierced, I pitched a fit to have mine done, too, but naturally my mother wouldn't hear of it.

"I'll worry about that later. Maybe I can hide it from her." I pulled Gretchen into the booth with me.

I picked out a pair of fourteen-karat gold studs and, while the lady prepared the gun that would blast the earrings I had chosen through my lobes, I sat in the chair with the same it's-out-of-my-hands-now feeling I once had when I was buckled into the first car on a roller coaster.

"Sure this won't hurt?" I asked Gretchen anxiously.

She shook her head. "Mine didn't hurt, much."

"The device works so fast you won't feel a thing," the lady assured me.

I closed my eyes. *Whomp!* The impact of the ear piercing gun was like being skewered with a hot wire. "Ow! You lied! I thought you said it wouldn't hurt!"

The lady looked concerned. "You're not going to faint, are you?"

Gretchen prevented me from leaping out of the chair. "Kobie, you can't leave now. She's not finished."

"Yes, she is!" My ear throbbed like a toothache.

"My dear, you can't go away with one ear pierced," the lady soothed. "Your lobes must be a little on the thick side. After you've rested a bit, we'll do the other one."

"Great," I groaned. "First, I've got rotten tonsils. Now I have fat earlobes. Okay, I guess I'm ready." I braced myself. *Whomp!* The second blow nearly drove me through the wall of the booth. Now both ears were killing me.

The lady collected the remainder of my Christmas money. "Come back in an hour. I'll see if there's any bleeding."

Numbly I wobbled out of the stall, my ears feeling as if they were clamped in a vise.

"Kobie, your ears are red as a beet," Gretchen remarked unnecessarily. Every dram of blood in my body must have been flooding my ears. "You'll never hide this from your mother."

"My whole head is busting! All I wanted was pretty gold earrings like Juliet. Instead I feel like I've got spikes jammed in the center of my brain. Plus all my Christmas money is gone, every last penny!" I wailed. "I don't know what came over me. Yes, I do! It's your fault, Gretchen Farris."

"My fault!"

"If we had eaten when we were supposed to, I wouldn't have given in to the temptation. What am I going to *do*?"

Of course, there was no answer to that question. The deed was done. My ears were pierced and there was no way I could unpierce them.

Impending doom (mine) apparently pushed Gretchen into action. While waiting for my last hour on earth to be up, she bought the gray sweater and the Snoopy golf trophy for Doug. Despite my pain, I came close to bopping her over the head with a blunt object. If she had bought those stupid presents when she first saw them, I wouldn't have blown my Christmas savings on pierced ears and earrings and would have more than a few hours to live.

Back at the Piercing Pagoda, the lady instructed me to turn my earrings and to swab the holes with alcohol until they were healed.

"I'll send you a postcard from reform school," I told Gretchen.

"Come on, Kobie. It's not that bad." For her it wasn't. After all, *her* mother had encouraged her to get pierced ears.

"Are you kidding? I bet she's getting my suitcase down from the attic right now."

"Look, there's one of those photograph booths," Gretchen exclaimed. "I've got exactly one dollar left. I'm going to have pictures of myself made for Doug."

Gretchen primped like a movie star preparing for a press conference. "Do I look okay?"

"Gorgeous. Hurry up. Your brother will be here any minute."

The orange curtain fluttered behind her. I studied the sample photos pasted on either side of the doorway. Where did they get such dorky pictures? And how come nobody cut up in them the way Gretchen and I used to when we took them on the boardwalk at Ocean City?

The light flashed for Gretchen's first picture, making me feel nostalgic for those wonderful days on the beach. Our families hadn't rented the beach house last July, the first summer we'd missed in years, because Gretchen had summer school. The second light flashed. I thought of how much we had changed. Sure, we were still best friends, but there seemed to be a gap between us, a chasm that was getting wider and wider. I was never very good at the broad jump. If Gretchen didn't look back soon and give me a hand across, I'd be left behind forever.

Gretchen's third picture was over. Suddenly I had an urge to recapture a little of our carefree past, bring back those long summers at the beach.

I stormed through the curtain. Gretchen

squealed, "Kobie, what are you doing?"

"What does it look like? Move over," I said, squeezing beside her on the bench. I had forgotten how little those booths were inside. Either that or we had gotten a lot bigger.

I grimaced at the hidden camera. "Come on, Gretch. Ham it up. This is the last shot." We always mugged on the final shot.

Giggling, Gretchen pushed up her nose and pulled down her bottom eyelids with one hand, her old standby Pekingese face. I twisted my mouth, stuck out my tongue, and crossed my eyes just as the flash went off.

When the processed strip dropped into the basket, still damp, Gretchen snatched it out. "Oh, Kobie, look at us!" We both screamed with laughter.

"That's our best gross picture yet!" I said. "Somebody ought to elect this to the Horrible Picture Hall of Fame. We look just like we did a few years ago."

"Yes, we do, don't we?" Gretchen agreed. Then she frowned at the studio-perfect poses of herself alone. "Which one should I have framed for Doug? The first one — no, maybe the third. My ring shows up better in that one, don't you think?"

She put the picture strip in her purse and we walked back to the aviary court to wait for her brother.

Chapter 10

"I asked my mother if I could get my ears pierced and she said no," Sandy remarked at lunch one day. "We don't have the money, she said."

"That's my mother's answer for anything I want," I replied. "Even if I want something that's *free* she claims we don't have the money. Of course, you can't believe them. Grown-ups work. They get a paycheck. But they think we still fall for that old line. Can I have your bread?"

Sandy was generously dividing her lunch with me. Half her Salisbury steak, half the potatoes, half the corn which she was laboriously counting kernel by kernel to make sure she wouldn't cheat me. I couldn't afford to buy my lunch this week or next week either. Since I had squandered my Christmas savings at the Piercing Pagoda, I was hoarding my lunch money to buy my mother and father a Christmas present. I was forced to rely on the kindness of strangers or starve.

Sandy pushed a gravy-soaked napkin over to me. "If you want more, just take it off my plate, but it should be even."

"It couldn't be more even if you had used a computer." But I ate hungrily.

"I'm dying to have pierced ears," Sandy said wistfully. "Then I'll be just like you."

"Do you want a prison uniform and a number around your neck just like me, too?"

"Your mother didn't get that upset."

Actually, she didn't. And my mother's basic reaction to my little adventures was well-known; it would have made the six o'clock news. When I came home from the mall with inflamed ears, new gold earrings, and guilt blazoned across my face, my mother did not rant and scream and lecture as I expected.

Instead she froze me with an icy stare and said only, "I'm disappointed in you, Kobie," before launching into a chilly description of the effects of blood poisoning, evidently the direct result of disobeying your mother and spending your Christmas money on yourself.

"I don't know why you girls are so anxious to get holes in your earlobes," Eddie Showalter said, shading the wings of a DC-9 he was drawing in the margin of his science book. Then, with a quick apologetic glance at me, he added, "Except your earrings look nice, Kobie."

"Thanks, but I'm paying for them dearly." I gobbled my half of Sandy's lunch so I could get to work. Because of my cash flow problem, I was drawing sketches from *Lady and the Tramp* to give as Christmas presents. For my mother, the spaghetti dinner scene I let Stuart have; and for my father, a scene outside Tony's restaurant, where the two dogs go for their date, both pictures duplicated from my portfolio. At the end of two lunchless weeks, I thought I'd have enough money to buy picture frames.

Eddie admired the Tony's restaurant sketch. "This is really good. The way you've got the light from the windows falling into the street."

"I must have done that over a hundred times," I confessed. "Lighting is so hard to do."

"Did you hear about Gretchen?" Sandy asked before Eddie and I lapsed into artist's talk.

"If you mean Patty Binninger's party, I've heard more about it than I want to." The story I had given my mother about Gretchen having a New Year's Eve party had come true, sort of. Gretchen wasn't having a party, but she and Doug had been *invited* to one at Patty Binninger's house, leaving you-know-who to stay at home wearing emerald velvet and lace ruffles.

"Maybe you'll get your invitation today," Eddie said. "Patty's in my science class. She's still asking people."

"And maybe the Queen of England is really my cousin," I said sadly. "Patty is only asking *couples* to her party, *popular* couples."

"Kobie's right," Sandy agreed. "Patty is awful stuck-up. In gym the other day I was trying to fix my hair and she butt right in front of me, like I wasn't even there."

"That's the way it is with those girls. We don't exist, according to them." I fished a piece of Aspergum, cleverly disguised in a regular chewing gum wrapper, from my purse. To add to my other woes, I had tonsillitis again. I hadn't told my mother yet, figuring she'd blame this new attack on my stupid ears.

"Can I have some?" Sandy held out her hand.

I could hardly refuse her, not after she'd donated half her lunch to Feed Kobie Roberts Week. She unwrapped the gum and popped it in her mouth. Aspergum wouldn't hurt her, just make her throat a little numb. I waited for Eddie to ask for a piece too, but when he didn't, I put the pack in

114

by purse, hoping he wouldn't think I was stingy. I really needed the stuff for my throat.

"New Year's Eve isn't everything," he said, still locked in the old conversation. Sometimes Eddie was slow. "My folks just stay home and watch that special TV program until midnight."

"So do mine," Sandy said.

Mine didn't even do that. "It's just a night like any other night," my father always said before going to bed at his regular time. I was probably the only living soul in the United States who has never seen the celebration in Times Square.

"We throw a big eggnog party — " I started to lie when Sandy grabbed my arm.

"Look! Isn't that Stuart? And *Rosemary Swan?* What are *they* doing together?"

I blinked twice. Stuart Buckley and Rosemary Swan, big as life at the next table. Stuart was actually helping Rosemary sit down without yanking the chair out from under her, the way he did to me one time. He hovered around her like a head waiter, unloading her tray, unfolding her napkin. I was surprised he didn't taste her food or open her milk carton.

"What a disgusting spectacle." I made vomiting motions. "Stuart's gone over the edge."

"What's he see in her?" Sandy wanted to know.

"What's she see in *him*, you mean." I wondered how Stuart managed to snag fickle Rosemary. He was certainly having better success with her than I was with T.E. My true love avoided me. At first I couldn't believe it, that a teacher would actually run away from a student, but he changed course whenever he saw me coming. Sandy said his love for me was evident and the look on his face was one of anguished torment. His facial expression looked more like irritation to me, but you never could tell with this love business.

"Stuart must be a riot," Sandy said. Rosemary was laughing so hard she could barely eat.

I watched them glumly, faintly aware of a strange emotion — could it be *jealousy?* Ever since Stuart asked me for my drawing, I kind of thought he might be interested in *me*. Not that I would consider going out with him for a minute. Yet all those questions he pestered me about — what girls like in boys and what did I think of him — he could have been pretending to like Rosemary as a trick to find out how *I* felt about him. At least, that's what I thought.

"Cheer up," Eddie said. "Christmas is coming."

As it turned out, I had little reason to be cheerful, Christmas or no Christmas. I went back to the doctor for my tonsillitis, which was so bad this time, swallowing brought new levels in pain. Dr. Wampler told my mother that my infections might get worse if my rotten tonsils didn't come out soon, but he agreed with my mother that we could wait a while longer before making a decision. For a second there, I thought he was going to take them out right in his office.

My mother mellowed again, fixing me custards and soups, the pierced ear incident apparently forgiven. Christmas Eve was a real bummer. I was too sick to decorate the tree. From the couch, I directed my mother in the correct placement of the ornaments, but she didn't follow orders very well and kept wanting to put my grandmother's star-shaped bulb near the bottom of the tree instead of near the top where it belonged, and drape the tinsel strand by strand rather than flinging it over the branches. As a result, our tree had an overdone, lopsided appearance.

When my father came home, he pronounced our tree lots nicer than the national Christmas tree and handed me a sack of my favorite old-fashioned peppermint sticks. I couldn't eat the candy, which depressed me so much I refused to join my parents in our Christmas Eve ritual of opening one gift each. Instead I sulked in the glow of the twinkling lights, feeling extremely sorry for myself and positive I was the only sick person on the planet. Fifteen, at last, and I was having the rottenest year imaginable.

Christmas Day was even worse. My parents had their traditional oyster stew for breakfast. Sitting across from those disgusting gray lumps bobbing in milk at seven in the morning was hard enough to take in good health. My mother also served French toast, which was too tough for me to swallow, so I had that most festive of all Christmas dishes, oatmeal.

Usually I wolf down breakfast so I can descend on the pile of presents heaped under the tree, but this year I shambled into the living room, coughing, and pulling my bathrobe around me. Listlessly, I opened my presents. My mother got me black patent leather pumps and a matching purse, plus white lacy stockings to wear with my fancy dress.

"I thought you were going to Gretchen's party," she said. "But Clare tells me she isn't having a party. Doug is taking her to some girl's house in Annandale."

"Patty Binninger's," I sniffed. "She's having the party, not Gretchen. And I wasn't invited."

"You're too sick to think about going out next week anyway."

My father's gift was a real surprise: a leather-cased manicure set. I stared at the gleaming implements neatly tucked into elastic straps.

"This is great! I love it. And it goes with Sandy's present." Sandy had given me the pale pink lipgloss and nail polish from the *Seventeen* ad, the one that inaugurated my ruffles-and-ribbons campaign to win T.E.

My father was unwrapping his present from me, a package that had the same suspicious shape as my mother's from me. "You're growing up more every day. I thought you could use something to make your fingernails pretty."

My fingernails were hopelessly stubby and, unless the kit contained a magic growth potion, they would remain that way despite my arsenal of cuticle pushers and nail buffers. But I kissed my father and told him again how much I adored his present.

Both he and my mother acted pleased with their framed sketches, my mother going so far as to take down the Spanish dancer prints on either side of the fireplace and hang up my pictures. Still, I felt shabby. I had received wonderful, grown-up presents, yet I had resorted to giving dowdy homemade gifts, because I had greedily spent my Christmas money on myself.

"Homemade presents are the best kind," my father said.

"Anybody can run out and buy something," my mother put in, "but making something takes time and thought."

I shuffled back to my couch, unable to eke out the teeniest feeling of goodwill from my shriveled, un-Christmasy heart.

Gretchen breezed by on her way to have Christmas dinner at Doug's. She burst into our too-warm living room, wreathed in a new mohair muffler and bringing in draughts of crisp, cold air. After wishing my parents a happy holiday and giving my mother a fruitcake from her mother, she handed me a tiny white box.

By then I had dissolved into a jellied mass of self-pity. Two frail tears trickled down my cheeks.

"Gretchen," I whispered, though I talked normally and even yelled at my mother up to the instant Gretchen had walked in, "I didn't get you anything. I didn't have any money. It was all I could do to scrape together enough to buy picture frames."

"So I'm one up on you," she said. "Now I'm ahead of you for the first time since second grade. Open it!"

Inside, anchored to a puff of cotton, was a pair of tiny silver hoops.

"They're beautiful! Where did you get them?"

She grinned at my pleasure. "International Bazaar. Doug helped me pick them out. See what he gave me?" She lifted her leg to display a delicate silver chain clasped around her stockinged ankle. "An ankle bracelet. Isn't it neat?"

The sight of such an intimate gift made me choke with envy. When I could speak, I said something crummy. "A *slave* bracelet. That's what they call those. He's your master and you're his slave."

"Kobie! What's the matter with you? It's an ankle bracelet, that's all."

"I'm sorry," I said, and meant it. "It's very pretty. Did Doug like his sweater?"

"He's supposed to be wearing it today."

"Oh, that's right. You're going to his house for dinner. Well, I hope you have a nice time."

"Doug says his folks are dying to meet me. Gotta run. Charles is waiting." She said good-bye to my folks and dashed back out again.

By New Year's Eve I was better, but my fate had already been decided. "Make the best of it," my mother suggested.

I spent the evening alone in my room, working on the final sketch for my Lady and the Tramp portfolio, a background scene of a Victorian house, elaborate with carving and towers, steeped in snow. It was the most ambitious picture in my whole portfolio, the showcase picture that would land me a job when I arrived in Burbank, California, two years from now.

Listening to the radio countdown of the Top 100 songs of the year helped pass the time. I wrote them down in my notebook as the dj announced each song, and made a private bet with myself which song would be number one. My fancy dress, starched and pressed, hung from the doorframe of my closet, the new patent leather pumps positioned beneath.

As the evening dragged on, it grew darker outside and I quit drawing because I didn't feel like switching on the lamp. Crouched in the dim light of the radio dial, I thought about Gretchen and Doug at Patty Binninger's. My white lace dress glowed eerily in the half-light, like the ghost of a young girl who had missed a long-ago New Year's Eve party.

Chapter 11

I was informed of Stuart's deceit during our first week of driver's ed.

"Rosemary was showing everybody that card in homeroom," Sandy announced, keeping a watchful eye out for the teacher. "I accidentally kicked my pen under Rosemary's desk so I could get a better look. It was two dogs eating spaghetti, just like the picture you were drawing for your mother. Stuart had made it like a card with a poem inside and signed his name. I couldn't read the poem, but that was his signature, all right."

Now I knew why Stuart hadn't wanted me to sign my drawing. "Worth more," indeed. The little rat planned to pass off my picture as his own the whole time.

"What are you going to do?" Sandy asked.

"I don't know yet. Boil him in oil,

maybe. No, that's too fast. The end ought to be slow and excruciating."

"Girls!" Miss Barlow glared at me and Sandy. "Are you paying attention? We're going to have a test and I expect you both to make A's."

Miss Barlow was expecting a lot. Despite a burning desire to learn how to drive, neither Sandy nor I were getting much out of classroom driver's training. So far we had both flunked a quiz based on state driving laws. We studied the pamphlet backward and forward, but all those regulations eluded us. Questions like, "When you are making a left turn, do you (a) signal, look in the mirror, then move over to the left of the center line when traffic allows, (b) signal and get over as quickly as possible, or (c) throw up your hands and hope that your car will somehow manage to drift into the left lane."

Sandy poked me with her pencil. "How many feet in a car length?"

"You're asking me? My driving information is mixed up with my mother's hysteria when she learned to drive last year. All I know is when you back out of a Seven-Eleven lot, you do *not* hit the sheriff, who might be walking behind your car just then."

"Your mother did that?"

I nodded. "Luckily, the sheriff jumped

out of the way or he would have been a
goner. He could have had her permit re-
voked, but I guess he felt sorry for her.
He told Mom when she got her license to
let him know and he'd stay off the road the
days she was out."

Gretchen was using the simulator. We
all had to practice braking. From my seat
in the back, I could see Gretchen's right
foot pouncing from the gas to the brake
pedals as she stared at the "windshield,"
actually a projection screen playing a
movie. The movie made it seem like you
were driving down a real street, passing
houses and stuff, when all of sudden a
child's ball would appear and you were
supposed to stop.

I was so bad that I hated to think how
many rubber balls I hit and innocent kids
I nearly ran down.

Gretchen braked correctly every time,
the silver ankle chain winking in the sun
as she pumped first one pedal and then the
other.

"Very good, Gretchen," Miss Barlow
commented. High praise from a teacher
who inscribed "Try to do better next time"
on papers with perfect marks.

Gretchen returned to her seat in front
of me, her face flushed from the compli-
ment. "Boy, this driving is harder than I
thought."

"At least you didn't come away with a record like I did."

"You'll catch on, Kobie," she said, confident because she had done so well.

Beside me, Sandy ripped a page from her driver's ed notebook, labeled "Sondra K. Robertson," and wrote, *I know how to get T.E.'s home address. Interested?*

I wrote back, *Does the sun rise in the east?*

Meet me at the main office before sixth, she replied.

Three periods from now. Fine with me. I still had a score to settle with a creepy little art swindler.

Stuart ambled into French, whistling. Rosemary towered over him. They made a comical couple, like Mutt and Jeff. After repeated reprimands from Mrs. Hildebrandt, he finally tore himself away from Rosemary's side.

He plopped down in his own desk and sighed happily. "Great day, isn't it, Kobie?"

I didn't answer.

"The crocuses are coming up in the courtyard," he rattled on. "Rosemary and I went out to see them at lunchtime. The juniors put benches out there. It'll be strictly a senior courtyard next year so you ought to go while you can."

I stared stonily at my French book.

He tugged a lock of my hair, trying to tease me into a smile. "Ko-bee. Are you in there? Look at your old friend Stuart. Come on."

Turning my head, I glowered at him so hard my eyes hurt.

He withdrew his hand swiftly, frightened I might bite him. "What a face! Better watch out, it could freeze that way."

I compressed my vision into twin lasers, riveting Stuart to the spot. I hoped to vaporize the little weasel into a confession.

"Quit staring at me like that. What's bugging you?"

"I think you know."

"I *don't* know."

"Don't play dumb, Stuart. I know why you asked for my drawing, unsigned. You made it into a card for Rosemary and she thinks *you* drew the picture."

He shrugged. "Yeah, so what?"

"So *what?*" Was there no limit to Stuart's nerve? Next he'd be forging my name on checks. "You told me you wanted one of my drawings as a keepsake. You didn't say anything about giving it to the Amazon Queen. That was a dirty, underhanded, double-dealing trick and I have a good mind to tell Rosemary the truth."

Stuart actually appeared jittery. "You're not, are you, Kobie? You wouldn't do that to me? Rosemary has just started to like me. You wouldn't ruin it for me by squealing, would you?"

"No," I said after a minute. "I won't say a word, Stuart."

"Great! You're just terrific, Kobie. I always knew you were!"

What Stuart didn't know was that Just Terrific Kobie wasn't going to say a word to *him* again. He had really hurt me with this betrayal and I wanted nothing to do with Stuart Buckley as long as I lived.

Sandy was waiting for me outside the main office. "You stay here," she said. "I'll only be a sec." She disappeared into the office, leaving me to hang around the bulletin board.

I felt T.E.'s presence before I actually saw him. His back was to me as he studied the basketball schedule. I feasted my eyes on him, shamelessly drinking in every detail, the blond highlights in his hair, the softness of his powder-blue sweater, the way his slacks broke over the instep of his loafers, just so. How could anyone that gorgeous breathe and walk around like the rest of us mortals?

Then, as if sensing me, he turned around. His expression went from uncertainty to concern as he recognized me. Without so much as a nod, he stepped into the office, practically running into Sandy, who was coming out.

"I got it!" She waved a slip of paper. "Did you see T.E.'s face just now? He's weakening, Kobie. He'll soon be yours."

I wasn't so sure about that.

"I also got his first name," Sandy said. "Want to hear it? Harold!"

"Harold? Harold Brown? Are you sure that's *my* Mr. Brown?" Harold wasn't at all manly, like Andrew or Montgomery. Harold wasn't a name that went with turquoise eyes. Still, T.E. couldn't help what his parents named him.

"There's only one Mr. Brown who teaches ninth-grade shop," Sandy said. "And he lives at 415 Sycamore in Fairfax."

Four-fifteen Sycamore, an elegant-sounding address, even if his name *was* Harold. I had to see T.E.'s house. Just knowing where he lived would bring him closer to me.

It took every ounce of my powers, but I lured Gretchen away from Doug Saturday morning with a trumped-up excuse that we *had* to go to the library. Charles drove us.

I had diligently studied my father's map the night before to pinpoint the exact location of T.E.'s street. Halfway there I told Charles, "I know a shortcut. Take a right here and we'll wind up in back of the library."

"But this road goes *away* from the library," Charles protested, turning right anyway. Gretchen's brother was neat. If I had to choose an older brother, it would be somebody like Charles. Although he took classes at NOVA, the community college, he had a wonderful tolerance for the whims of sophomore girls.

"This street," I said, pointing. "Turn here, on Sycamore."

Gretchen flashed me her fishy eye. I hadn't filled her in on my scheme, but I think she figured what I was up to. We'd been friends too long not to understand how each other's brains worked.

"You sure this comes out at the library?" Charles coasted down the residential lane.

I was busy looking at the house numbers. Then I spied *his* house, a brick bungalow with green awnings. His station wagon was parked in the driveway, a couple of metal garbage cans were stacked just outside the front gate. How domestic and cozy. It was even better than elegant. Any second T.E. could come out and pick up his newspaper and he'd see me . . . *riding* down his street. Suddenly, it was vital that I *drive* past his house. When he came out, I didn't want to be slumped in the backseat like a little kid.

"Charles!" I screeched, startling him so he nearly ran up on the sidewalk. "Let me drive!"

"What? Are you nuts? You don't know how to drive."

"Yes, I do!" Never mind that Miss Barlow had tagged me Menace of the Highway. "You give Gretchen steering lessons. Won't you give me one? My parents won't let me use their precious old car." That was true. Whenever I mentioned taking a ride to show off my new skills, my father made noises about not having enough insurance.

Charles sighed, weakening. "Kobie, if anything happens to you and Gretchen I'm responsible — " I knew why he was leery. Two years ago he was driving on a rain-slicked road when the car hit a tree and caused Gretchen to hurl through the windshield. Gretchen said even now Charles sweated bullets when he gave her steering lessons in their driveway.

"Nothing will happen," I said. "I'm just going to drive to that stop sign. Just that short distance. That's all."

"All right," Charles relented. He put the car in park but left the engine running while we switched places. Gretchen climbed into the backseat. She didn't say a word, but I could feel disapproval radiating from her.

I gripped the wheel like a life preserver while Charles adjusted my seat so I could reach the floor controls. I still had trouble seeing over the dash. If I didn't grow and *soon*, my driving days would be confined to go-carts and tricycles.

"Put your foot on the clutch," Charles instructed, "put it into first, then let the clutch out slowly as you accelerate."

"Could you run that by me again?"

"I thought you said you practiced this."

"Oh, I have," I replied, indicating I had been driving straight-stick since infancy. With my left foot, I fumbled with the pedals on the floor, struggling to remember if our classroom simulator even had a clutch pedal.

"That's the brake," Charles said.

"I know! I'm just making sure it works. Uh, which way is first?"

He leaned over and pushed the gearshift lever over and down a notch. "Kobie, I think you'd better forget this today."

"No! I'm okay. This car is different from my — from the one I'm used to, is all."

"Gearboxes are the *same* in cars with manual transmissions. You're in first. Put the clutch to the floor and let it out slow — "

I jammed the pedal to the floor and let it out with a jerk. The car idled forward about a centimeter, then stalled. Scared out of my wits, I screamed, "What'll I do?"

Charles rolled his eyes skyward. "Start the engine and try again."

I turned the key too far and the engine made a horrible grinding sound. Charles looked as if he might cry and I didn't blame him. His car was his pride and joy.

"Sorry." This time when I let out the clutch and the car coughed, preparing to stall, I pounded the clutch to the floor again, preventing the engine from dying.

"The gas!" Charles yelled. "Give it some gas. Let off the clutch!"

I *couldn't* let off the clutch. My foot had developed a will of its own, jackhammering the clutch to the floor, then jerking back like a piston, slamming, jerking, until the car bucked like a bee-stung bronco.

Finally the car panted to a halt, undoubtedly exhausted. We had progressed a grand total of twelve inches. I felt like I had just spent a month in a blender.

Charles was opening the passenger door. "Kobie, let's do this some other time. You really aren't — "

I bobbed up and down in the driver's seat. "Please, Charles! Let me try again. I think I have it now. Please, give me another chance!"

"Come on, Charles." Gretchen loyally came to my defense. "Let her try again. I haven't had this much fun since the county fair last summer."

Charles closed the door. "Three strikes and you're out, Kobie. We'll try it once more. Get your foot on the *gas*. That's what makes a car go."

This time I would drive smoothly past

T.E.'s house, showing the love of my life my professional technique. "He just has to see me," I muttered to myself.

"It's February," Gretchen said, linked to my train of thought as always. "Why would he be outdoors?"

"Then maybe he'll see me from the window."

"Eyes on the road!" Charles shouted. "Clutch to the floor, Kobie, ease it out at the same time giving it some gas."

I squashed the pedal to the floor but as I started to let it out, the car trembled, wanting to cut off again. Whipping my foot off the clutch, I hit the gas so hard the wheels spun and laid a strip of smoking rubber. The car bounded forward with a bone-jarring lurch. The three of us sat terrified as we bore down on 415 Sycamore with the speed of a runaway locomotive. All I could think was that the love of my life would certainly get a good look at me as we plowed into his living room.

The car steamrolled over something crunchy, as if the grill were being chewed in a meat grinder. Charles reached over and shut off the ignition.

"We just demolished that man's trash cans," he reported gloomily. "Not to mention the tires and drive shaft of my car. When you strike out, Kobie Roberts, you *really* strike out."

Chapter 12

"Stuart tells me you're not speaking to him," Gretchen said a few days later in typing. She shifted the carriage to check the letter Mrs. Antle had just dictated to us at machine-gun velocity.

"That's right, I'm not," I said. "Why should I, after what he did?"

"I know what he did was terrible, but aren't you carrying this revenge thing too far? That was ages ago."

"A true friend doesn't betray another friend," I said loftily. "I can stand anything but dishonesty."

"I never realized you were so hard-nosed, Kobie. I always thought you were easygoing."

"Not any more." I cranked the platen of my typewriter to look over my own letter. *dearmrjones*, I had typed. *thisisinresponsetoyourtelephonecalloflastfriday* —

Mrs. Antle had dictated so fast, I didn't have time to capitalize or put in spaces. I could almost see the glee on Mrs. Antle's face as she scratched a big fat D- on my paper.

"Darn." Gretchen frowned. "I transposed twice. Typos count ten points."

I mentally revised my D- into a graphline that dived off the chart. My mother had suggested that I take business courses. "You can always be a secretary," she said last summer when we were planning my classes. "I know my little girl has her heart set on going to college, but we simply can't afford it, Kobie, unless you win a scholarship."

Actually, her little girl's heart was set on going to Walt Disney Studios in Burbank, California, approximately twelve seconds after graduation. I went along with my mother, believing I could get a job for a few weeks as a secretary until I earned enough to buy an airplane ticket to California. Now, adding up the jillions of typos in my letter, I realized my job opportunities would be severely restricted to bosses who didn't speak English, began every letter with "This is in response to your telephone call of last Friday," and were, in addition, a little soft in the head.

Gretchen glanced over at my paper. "Your space bar get stuck or what?"

I didn't answer. Today, despite my troubles in typing, I felt very self-contained. I knew exactly what I was doing. I wasn't bothered by Stuart's feeble attempts to talk me into making up. I didn't even care that Gretchen hardly ever called me anymore; I had finally accepted her as more or less a permanent attachment to Doug McNeil.

My newfound peace was due to a secret plan. By second period tomorrow, T.E. would pledge his love to me. I was banking on it.

"Absolutely not," my mother said the next morning. "You are not going to school wearing a skimpy party dress!"

"But, Mom, I *have* to. We're having Paris day in French and I'm supposed to be one of those runway models like they have in Paris fashion shows." The fib, concocted in bed last night, rolled out with practiced ease. I had chosen this day very carefully. It was February 14, Valentine's Day. The date, along with my party dress, were important parts of my plan.

"Well, you can be a Paris runway model in your red blouse and a skirt. You're not wearing that party dress to school and that's final, Kobie." She stalked off to reheat my breakfast.

All was not lost. I had too much at stake

to let a minor obstacle like my mother block my way. Humming, I brushed more "Iced Espresso" eyeshadow on my eyelids until my eyes looked sultry.

The lace dress skimmed over my head as I slipped it on. It felt deliciously light and cool, after I had been encased in layers of wool for so many weeks. From my pile of uglies next to my bureau I plucked out an awful button-down-the-front number and put it on over my party dress. The effect was lumpy, but I would get past my mother. I stuffed my white lace stockings in my purse, then dropped my black patent leather pumps in the deep pockets of my stadium coat.

"No time for breakfast," I told my mother.

"Kobie, what have you got on? That dress needs ironing."

"It needs dynamiting," I replied tartly. "If I can't wear my party dress to school, then I'm going looking as dowdy as possible. I hope you realize this means I can't be in the fashion show." I stomped out the door without saying good-bye.

The monkey wrench my mother tried to throw in my plan caused barely a ripple. Phase One had been accomplished with only a slight hitch. On the bus the second fib tripped off my tongue.

"I have an appointment with my counselor during first," I said to Gretchen, who clasped an enormous red cardboard heart on top of her books. Doug's Valentine, undoubtably. "Tell Mrs. Antle I'll bring her a note tomorrow." That is, if I was still in town. T.E. might impulsively swoop me off to the Caribbean.

I didn't reveal my plan to Gretchen. She probably wouldn't have cared. Sandy would have been avidly interested, but I hadn't told her, either, for a different reason. Sandy was a blabbermouth and my plan hinged on the element of surprise.

As soon as the bus hesitated by the curb, I catapulted myself into the school like a guided missile, aiming for the nearest girls' room. Locked in a stall, I unbuttoned the dress, stashed it behind the toilet, stripped off my regular hose and put on the lacy white stockings, traded my loafers for the patent leather pumps. Phase Two completed.

The image in the mirror over the sinks astonished me. A vision in white emerged from the stall, a living Valentine with a halo of curly hair, long coltish legs, big dark eyes. Plain old Kobie Roberts was transformed into the new, improved, and utterly romantic Kobie Roberts. T.E. was a sure goner. On to Phase Three.

I stayed in the bathroom until the late bell for first period rang. When I was certain classes had started, I walked to the industrial arts wing, my stomach fizzy with anticipation.

Someone had left open the big double doors that led to the outside unloading platform. A stiff winter breeze billowed the wispy sleeves of my dress. Chiffon, I discovered, was about as warm as cheesecloth, but even an arctic wind couldn't dent my sense of purpose. I marched to T.E.'s classroom with my head high, picturing his expression when he saw me. His turquoise eyes would bulge with disbelief, then fill with true love as he realized he couldn't deny it another instant. He might even propose without further delay.

Skilsaws whirred from behind the closed doors of T.E.'s shop class. I knocked, but evidently no one heard me over the racket. I knocked louder and a boy wearing safety goggles came to the door.

"Yeah?" he asked, unimpressed with my angelic finery.

"I have a message for T — I mean, Mr. Brown," I stammered.

"He's busy. What is it? I'll give it to him."

"No! I have to do it! I — it's personal." My throat suddenly felt lined in cotton.

The kid yelled, "Mr. Brown! Some girl here to see you!"

"Don't cut off any fingers until I get

back," a man's voice said. The door opened wider and there he was. "Can I help you?"

My heart stopped. Just stopped cold, like a conked-out battery. I had no idea what I was going to say. With all my detailed scheming, I had never planned what I would say to *him*. It ought to be something devastating, to go with my devastating outfit. Instead, I opened and closed my mouth like a fish out of water.

T.E.'s turquoise eyes did not bulge in amazement but the veins on his neck did. His face got redder than Gretchen's Valentine card. At first I thought he was blushing but then it occurred to me he was closer to having a stroke.

"You — !" he accused and I quaked, thinking he had recognized me as the culprit who ran over his garbage cans. "I just can't — " Abruptly he pushed past me, striding down the hall away from his class, and students in danger of slicing off their fingers, away from me.

I stood rooted to the floor.

"Boy," said the goggle-eyed kid. "That must have been some message."

His taunting words jarred me. I fled down the corridor to the open doors and out onto the delivery platform. In a flurry of flying lace, I leaped from the concrete dock to the grassy area between a parked milk truck and the building. Curled up against the bricks, my knees pressed to my chest, I let the sobs go.

What was the matter with T.E.? Why did he run like that? He acted as if the sight of me in my beautiful white dress was the straw that broke the camel's back. He was supposed to fall madly in love with me, as in forever till there is no end, not run away.

I cried until no more tears were left and my makeup was thoroughly smeared. I was half-frozen, but I didn't care. If only I could stay there the rest of the day. The rest of my life, even. How could I go back inside, knowing I had made such a fool of myself?

Practicality won. By the time the second-period bell shrilled, my teeth were clacking like castenets from my shivering. I considered faking a tonsillitis attack and calling my mother to come get me, but then she would see me in the very dress she'd expressly forbidden me to wear to school. No, I would have to return to my classes. Much as I wanted, I couldn't run away like T.E. had and I couldn't sit outside all day.

Feeling worse than the time last year when I was hauled back to school in a squad car, I brushed dirt off the tiers of ruffled lace and went back in. The old button-down-the-front dress I had stuffed behind the toilet in the girls' room was still there. I put it on over my party dress, splashed cold water on my face to rinse away the mascara streaks, then walked slowly to English.

I moved through my classes like a robot, ignoring barbs about my sack dress, refusing to participate in discussions, never volunteering answers. I skipped lunch and got a pass for the library instead, where I skulked behind the stacks. I didn't want to see anybody I knew, especially Sandy. After all, she had masterminded this whole romance business.

A ball of hate formed in the spot vacated by the warm feelings I'd had for T.E. I hated Sandy for getting me in trouble, and Stuart for being such a sneak, and my mother for her rules about dating, and Gretchen-and-Doug for being so much in love, and T.E. for destroying my dreams. Deep down inside, like a worm buried in an apple, I also hated myself.

A day already tainted by a rejection from my true love could not possibly get worse. Or so I thought.

I walked into math. I had dreaded this class most of all. T.E.'s shop class was just around the corner. Frequently, my algebra teacher and T.E. would be chatting in the hall.

Today, though, I didn't see either T.E. or my math teacher. The kids were antsy, wondering where Mr. Bell was. Sandy jabbed me in the back with the eraser end of her pencil.

"What's with you? You look terrible." I knew she meant the awful dress I had on over my party dress but was too tactful to come right out and say so.

"That's my natural state," I replied.

"How come you didn't show up for lunch? Eddie was worried about you."

"*Eddie* was worried? What about you? Weren't you worried?"

"Yeah, I was. You didn't speak to me or Gretchen in driver's ed. We've hardly seen you all day. What's up?"

"Nothing's up. In fact, it's all over. Between me and T.E. Your dumb idea didn't work. I don't know why I bothered listening to you."

"What are you talking about?" She poked me with her pencil eraser again, but I didn't respond.

Mr. Bell came in. "Sorry I'm late," he said. "I've been helping a friend with a problem." He picked up the attendance book, then slammed it back on his desk, obviously upset.

Mr. Bell was the kind of teacher who liked to share whatever was on his mind. On Mondays, he often told us what he did over the weekend. If he read an article in the *Post* that disturbed him, he confided his views to us.

Now he paced in front of the blackboard, as if wrestling over whether to tell us what was bothering him. A prickly sensation crawled along my arms. Suddenly I knew what he was going to say.

He sucked in a deep breath. The class was absolutely silent.

"This friend of mine is a teacher here in his first year of teaching," he began. "Nice young fella. For the longest time, this teacher has been chased by a young girl, a student. *Tormenting* him, for weeks. My friend isn't used to dealing with a situation like this. Today, something happened that really got to him. I've been in the lounge, advising him on how to handle the problem next time."

My whole body felt hot. That was *me* Mr. Bell was talking about. *I* was the young girl tormenting his friend. T.E. must have told Mr. Bell that the girl bothering him was in his sixth-period math class. Even if T.E. hadn't told him, all Mr. Bell had to do was look over and see guilt branded across my face!

"Who's the girl?" a boy asked.

"Who she is doesn't matter," Mr. Bell said, warming up to his subject. "What is important is this teacher's feelings. That girl didn't consider his feelings when she followed him around." What about *my* feelings? "I don't think you people realize how difficult it is for teachers — "

Sick to my stomach, I blotted out his speech. Sandy nudged me with her pencil, sharp persistent punches. I didn't turn around.

"That's you!" she whispered. "He's talking about *you*, isn't he?"

"Be quiet!"

"Kobie, I feel awful! I only wanted to fix you up with T.E. I never meant to get you in trouble."

"Forget it," I said out of the corner of my mouth.

"But you're mad at me."

"No, I'm not." I really wasn't, I decided. What happened today wasn't her fault. She didn't make me go to T.E.'s class dressed in white.

Mr. Bell's lecture about how sometimes students were inconsiderate to teachers droned on and on. I hunched my shoulder blades against his tirade, mortified to the core. I couldn't have been more humiliated if I had been put in stocks in the public square and flogged.

Chapter 13

If I kept a journal, I would have recorded that fifteen, the year things were supposed to get better, was the year I uncovered the Big Lie. Big Lies are myths made up by grown-ups. Peel away the soft, fluffy outer shell of these myths and you find a hard grain of truth.

The first Big Lie I unmasked was about love, that even if you love someone, there's no guarantee he will love you back. The second Big Lie concerned the old adage that when you have your tonsils removed, you can have all the ice cream you want. I had plenty of time to contemplate lies and truths, especially the ice cream one, from my bed in Prince William Hospital.

Thanks to the escapade on Valentine's Day, I came down with the worst case of tonsillitis ever, prompting Dr. Wampler to recommend surgery. My mother wanted to wait until Spring Break, but that was almost a month away. So this morning I was operated on and woke up, groggy and tonsil-less, about an hour ago, furious at being betrayed by an adult for the second time in a week.

"I don't *want* any," I whined in a cracked voice to my mother, who was trying to force-feed strawberry ice cream down my throat. "I can't swallow!"

"You can swallow this," she insisted. "It's soft and cool. It'll glide right down."

I had already tried some and hadn't liked it. Petulantly, I shoved the spoon aside. "I'm hungry. I want real food. I want a hamburger."

"Forget the hamburger." My mother set the ice cream dish on my over-the-bed tray with a clatter. "You can only have soft foods for a while, like custard and cereal. And nothing but ice cream today. Doctor's orders."

I flung myself back on the pillows. My throat felt raw and incredibly sore, but did I get any sympathy? No. Just somebody poking a bunch of dumb ice cream in my face and telling me I had to live on oatmeal the rest of my life. I wished I was dead. Then I looked over in the next bed and wished my roommate was dead.

When Dr. Wampler scheduled my operation, I dampened my panic with thoughts of rooming with a girl my age, someone who knew how tough it was being fifteen, grown-up but not allowed to do anything yet. I imagined the two of us sympathizing over our illnesses, cementing friendship over thermometers, the way Gretchen had made friends when she was in the hospital after her accident and during her plastic surgeries.

What I got was so far from what I had dreamed it wasn't funny. When I swam up from the thick, opaque ether sleep, the first thing I saw was a little girl with long sausage curls lying on the next bed, coloring in a coloring book. Then my eyes took in the television set suspended overhead, tuned to a cartoon program.

The girl stared at me. "She's awake," she said to other people in the room I hadn't noticed. She scooted across the bed, holding out an orange crayon. "Want to color? I'll let you do the Huckleberry Hound page. I saved it for you."

I turned to the wall and gagged.

"She's sick," I heard my mother say.

A nurse swished to my side and held a kidney-shaped pan under my chin. "It's the ether, honey," she reassured me. "What they used to put you to sleep. It sometimes upsets the tummy."

I wasn't nauseated from the anesthetic but from the sight of that girl offering me her Huckleberry Hound page. So much for sympathy.

"This is Beth Ann," my mother said. "She likes to be called Bethie."

What else? "What's she in here for?" I croaked. "She looks fine to me." Except for a terminal case of nerdiness.

"I'm having some tests. Now you're awake," Beth Ann chirped, "we can play."

I groaned, but not with pain.

Two facts I learned about Beth Ann: one, she was twelve years old, though she looked and acted about six; and two, my mother was infatuated with her. My mother had a fondness for nice little girls with long sausage curls.

Beth Ann's taste in television ran to Bugs Bunny and Daffy Duck and she laughed at everything including commercials. When she wasn't coloring for my mother, Beth Ann charmed her with tear-jerking stories about how she was an only child and had always wanted an older sister just like me.

Of course, the contrast between Beth Ann and me as patients was like night and day, with Beth Ann falling into the ideal patient category and rewarded by nurses and her roommate's mother fawning all over her. I was regarded as "difficult" and was taken care of grudgingly.

"Why can't you be sweet like Bethie?"

my mother chided after I pushed away the strawberry ice cream with such violence the dish skidded to the floor.

"I'd like to see how sweet you'd be after you had *your* tonsils out!" Hospitals and twelve-year-old girls with long curls made me grumpy.

"Everybody's mean to me," I whimpered. "The nurses don't like me."

"They do like you. It's just that they've never seen such a big baby before," my mother said. "Kobie, if you don't straighten up, I'm not staying here tonight."

She had arranged to have a cot brought in the room. Dr. Wampler told her it wasn't necessary for her to stay overnight, but she was scared I might choke or something and nobody would hear me. Given the attitude of the nurses, who were probably hoping I'd meet an untimely end, maybe it was best a relative spend the night with me. But I didn't want her to know that.

"Don't stay," I snapped. "I don't care."

"Kobie, you shouldn't talk to your mother like that," put in Pollyanna.

"Bethie has more sense than you do," my mother said.

"Will everybody leave me alone?" I threw the sheet over my head and tried to shut out the world.

The worst moment came at dinnertime. An orderly wheeled in a cart bearing two trays topped with metal covers. The wonderful aroma of spaghetti persuaded me to come out of my cocoon. I hadn't had solid food in years, it seemed. My mother propped up my bed so I could eat and rolled the over-the-bed tray closer.

Beth Ann sampled the entree with her pinkie finger. "Mmmmmm. Spaghetti! My favorite!"

I snatched the cover off my tray, but instead of tantalizing spaghetti and tomato sauce like Beth Ann's, I had a dish of glop, something pale green and half-melted, like a bar of soap scooped up from the bathtub drain. "What is *this*?"

My mother was digging the spoon into the gummy substance, preparing to feed me. "Lime Jell-O. I asked the doctor if you could have anything besides ice cream."

"What's *wrong* with it? It's runny."

"They let it soften a little," she replied. "Even regular Jell-O would be too hard for you to swallow. Now open up."

I wasn't opening up for anything green. "I want spaghetti!" I said, straining my vocal cords and my mother's patience to the limit.

"Stop it!" my mother hissed. "If you don't behave, I'm going home!"

I pushed the bowl off the tray, where it flipped over on my bed. Disgusted, my mother rang for the nurse, who cleaned up the mess with a tight-lipped if-that-was-*my*-kid-I-know-what-I'd-do-to-her look.

"Kobie's tired from her operation," Beth Ann said.

I despised Miss Goody-Two-Shoes making excuses for me. My throat throbbed, but my heart hurt worse. Dr. Wampler was able to snip out my rotten tonsils, but there wasn't any cure for a shattered heart.

Visiting hours began as the supper trays were being collected. I expected Pollyanna to have an endless stream of grandmotherly types ooh and aah over her, but surprisingly, the first visitor was for me.

Gretchen came in, bringing me a stuffed dog that looked like Tramp. My mother, relieved to escape from me, left us alone.

"I didn't expect to have company," I said, after thanking her for the dog.

Gretchen sat down in the visitor's chair. "I know how it is to be in a hospital, remember? I thought you could use cheering up. What pretty flowers."

The carnations and mums were from my father, delivered right after supper, but I found myself casually lying, "They're from T.E."

"Who? Oh, that teacher." Gretchen gave me her fishy eye. "Come on, Kobie. No teacher sent you those flowers."

"He did! He knew I was going in the hospital and he sent them!"

"If you say so. Before I forget, this is from Stuart." She handed me an envelope from her purse.

"What is it, a poison pen letter?" I held the envelope between two fingers, as if it might explode. "How did he know I was in here, anyway? Did you blab?"

Gretchen shook her head. "He doesn't know you're in the hospital. I just told him you were out sick."

The envelope contained a homemade card, a crude amateurish version of my *Lady and the Tramp* dinner scene. Inside was a poem: *Roses are red, Violets are dumb, Sorry I acted, Like such a crumb.*

"He didn't sign it," Gretchen said, reading over my shoulder.

I leaned the card against the water pitcher where I could see it. "It's worth more unsigned." This was the best get-well message I could have received. Stuart and I were friends again.

Gretchen rambled on about school, but seemed subdued.

"What is it?" I asked her.

For an answer, she drew the chain from underneath her sweater. Her precious gold and onyx ring was gone.

"You lost your ring?"

"No," she said. "Doug and I broke up."

I couldn't have been more thunderstruck if she told me she had enlisted in the Navy. "Broke up? But *why?*"

"We were seeing so much of each other. In school, out of school, phone calls every hour when we weren't together. I felt like — like he owned me." The image of her silver slave bracelet flashed through my brain. "I guess I missed hanging around with my friends, with you. Doing stuff in school. Doug was taking up my whole life."

"But you *loved* him. Doug was *the one.*"

"I don't know if he was or not, now." She paused. "I think I was more in love with the *idea* of being in love."

She wasn't the only one guilty of being in love with the idea of love. Maybe, just *maybe,* I manufactured the bolt of lightning in the background the first time I saw T.E. Even if I had been infatuated with him and not really in love, I still felt scarred.

"Does it hurt, since you gave Doug back his ring?"

Her blue eyes reflected a misty sadness. "Yeah. It does." She gathered up her purse. "I'd better go. Charles is waiting in the lobby. He said hi. You know how he is about hospitals. He hardly came to see me after my accident." Her wallet tumbled out on my bed.

I picked it up for her. In the plastic

window where a driver's license was supposed to go Gretchen had slipped in the goofy photo-booth picture of us, taken the day we went Christmas shopping. Something caught in my throat when I saw it. Such an honest, loyal gesture demanded equal honesty from me.

"Those flowers," I confessed. "My dad sent them."

"I know." She clasped my hand briefly and I realized there had never been any gap between us. We had different interests because we were individuals, but we were still best friends and probably would be forever.

About a half an hour after Gretchen left, my mother declared there was *a boy* to see me.

"A boy?" I sat up, wishing I was wearing something more glamorous than a hospital gown. My mother told whoever it was to come in, then went down to the nurse's station, confident that Beth Ann was more than capable as a chaperone.

Eddie Showalter entered the room, smiling shyly. "Hi, Kobie." One arm was hidden behind his back.

"Eddie! What are *you* doing here?"

"I came to see you." He presented me with a wilted bouquet of daisies. "These got a little limp. I guess they need water."

Cardiac resuscitation couldn't have revived those flowers.

"The florist was closed," he explained. "And so was the Giant supermarket. But out back they had a whole bunch of stuff they were throwing out. Out of all the flowers in the Dumpster, these were the best."

What, no dented canned goods? I started to ask, then bit back the remark. It was really very nice of Eddie to visit me in the hospital. "Thanks. I'll have the nurse put them in water," I said grandly, aware the nurses would rather assist Dracula than come near me. "How did you know I was in here?"

Eddie perched uncomfortably on the edge of the visitor's chair. "I asked Gretchen and she told me."

"She wasn't supposed to."

"Kobie, I knew you were sick. You'd come to school with your neck wrapped up in that scarf and were always chewing Aspergum . . . I had tonsillitis when I was eight. I remember like it was yesterday."

"Did you have your tonsils out?"

He nodded. "They said I could have all the ice cream I wanted but ice cream was so cold, it made my throat hurt worse."

"That's what I tried to tell my mother!" It was wonderful having someone who really *understood*. "If you knew I had tonsillitis, how come you kept quiet?"

"It was obvious you didn't want anyone to find out," he replied with a shrug. "I figured you had your reasons for coming to school sick and it wasn't my place to give you away."

Why hadn't I noticed how wide-set and sincere Eddie's brown eyes were? T.E.'s — *Harold's* — were too close together and a bit shifty besides.

A nurse announced that visiting hours were almost over. Eddie stood up so quickly, he banged into Beth Ann's tray-table. "I'll see you in school when you get back," he said.

"Okay. And thanks again for the flowers."

Eddie stuffed his hands in his pockets and gazed at the lamp over my bed. "Kobie — uh, maybe you and me could go out sometime? When you're all better?"

If I hadn't been lying down already, I would have swooned. "Gee, Eddie, I — " For once, words failed the Smartmouth. Then I recalled my mother's ironclad edict about dating. "I'd like to go out. Do you mind waiting five or six months?"

"Is it going to take you that long to get well?"

"No. I'm not allowed to date till I'm sixteen." I felt unbelievably infantile telling

158

him that. He left, probably wondering if I was old enough to cross the street by myself.

Beth Ann had been silent during Eddie's visit. When my mother came back, twitching with curiosity and ready to question me, Beth Ann piped, "That was a real nice boy, Mrs. Roberts. He asked Kobie out after she got better. I think you should let her."

Beth Ann's unsolicited opinion took the wind out of my mother's sails. "We'll see," was all she said.

I turned over, signaling I wanted to go to sleep. I had a lot to think about — Gretchen's startling news and Eddie's visit. My infatuation with T.E. But mostly I lay there thinking how the biggest lies are the ones we tell ourselves.

Chapter 14

I was out of school three weeks and then it was Spring Break, which meant I had an extra week to recuperate from my operation. My throat healed slowly and I lost eight pounds because it hurt so much to swallow. Now I didn't even resemble a coatrack.

"Dr. Wampler said it's natural to lose a few pounds," my mother assured me, mixing up yet another calorie-laden milk shake. "I know your throat is sore, but you have to eat."

"I'm just not hungry," I told her, day after day, meal after meal. And I wasn't.

I spent a lot of time in my room, listening to the hum of my empty fish tank and doing the homework assignments Sandy and Gretchen called in to me. My mind spun free, like a bicycle wheel, and when I closed my eyes to rest I saw nothing but white space behind my eyelids.

One afternoon, I lay on my bed watching the first robins dotting our backyard. I wondered if the birds had returned after a winter vacation or if they led two separate lives, one in the north, the other in the south, with no ties to either place. Most of the robins were paired off. How did the birds find their mates? Was there an even number of male robins and female robins born each year? Somehow I doubted it — life was seldom that fair.

I picked up my physical science book, but I knew the answer: There were left-over birds just as there were leftover people, and I was one of them. I didn't fit in anywhere.

My mother came in with a tray. She'd become a regular Florence Nightingale since my surgery. "What's wrong?" she asked, looking at my face. "Are you sick?"

No more than usual, I felt like replying. I showed her the page in my science book where the girl had written, *I love Mike still as in forever till there is no end.*

"Will I ever feel this way about anybody? Will anybody feel this way about *me?*"

My mother sat down on my bed and brushed my bangs off my forehead. "Someday someone will. Falling in love is a wonderful experience."

Falling in love with T.E. had been anything but wonderful. I was tempted to tell her about my crush on the shop teacher, but decided the wound was too raw.

"But it won't happen this year or in your junior year or probably not even in high school," she continued. "You have to be emotionally ready to fall in love and you're too young right now."

But not too young to be hurt. I twisted the bedcovers around my ring finger.

"Kobie, why are you moping around so?" my mother said. "You sit in this room all the time . . . you don't even play that awful record anymore. Having your tonsils out isn't the end of the world. What's bothering you?"

I sighed. "I thought this was going to be such a good year, that things would really get better. But they haven't. The year is practically over and I'm still not popular. I didn't learn to drive. I got sick. I'm not having any *fun*."

"Life isn't always fun, but it *is* what you make it."

My mother could always be depended on to produce one of her mottos. *You made your bed, now you lie in it* was one that had nothing to do with cleaning my room. *Life is what you make it* was trotted out whenever I was at my lowest, like now, as if my misery was my own doing.

"Life *isn't* what you make it," I argued. "I tried to make things happen, like learning to drive and getting in the popular crowd, but it didn't work. Nothing ever goes right for me. I don't even know why I'm here."

Mom smiled. "Because your father and I wanted you, that's why. I don't like to see my little girl unhappy. What would you like to do? Go shopping? Have the girls over for another slumber party?"

"I want to go out on a date," I blurted. "With Eddie Showalter. He's already asked me to see *Fantasia*, this old Walt Disney movie that's an animated classic. Can I go?"

The strangest expression came into my mother's eyes, as if she realized the ground we had gained so precariously these last few weeks was shifting again.

It was her turn to sigh. "You know the rule, Kobie, and you won't be sixteen until July." Before I opened my mouth to protest, she went on. "Remember I told you how my mother wouldn't let me date until I was eighteen? I thought my mother was terribly unfair. All my friends were going to church socials with boys and I had to stay home. I loved my mother, but I resented her rule."

"Just like *I* resent your rule." I had lost before the battle began.

"Resent the rule, but don't resent me. I'm only doing what I think is best for you. But rules aren't set in concrete, which is why — " and here the earth stood still " — if it's okay with your father, I'm going to allow you to go out *this once*."

"I can go!" I shrieked. "I can really go!"

"Yes, you can go — but *only* according to my rules."

My movie date with Eddie was contingent upon so many restrictive clauses, I felt like a prisoner let out on good behavior. *Only* the early show on Saturday was acceptable and we could stay out afterward *only* an hour to get a snack and that was *only* if we were accompanied by a responsible adult. Eddie had to come in when he picked me up and meet my parents formally and probably sign an affadavit that he would have me back no later than six-thirty. Eddie's father volunteered to be the responsible adult.

Friday, the day before the Big Event, my mother came back from the store with a bag from Robert Hall.

"None of your clothes fit anymore," she said, "so I bought you this to wear tomorrow."

The new dress, a tiny purple and brown checked fabric, had a dropped waist and a short flounced skirt. The high neckline and elbow-length sleeves hid my jutting collar-bone and skinny arms. I twirled in front of the mirror. With my lacy stockings and new black pumps I would look — well, not like Juliet, but not too bad.

"Will Eddie think I'm an enchanting creature?" I asked my mother. I always wanted to be called an enchanting creature. "Or will he think I'm just a creature?"

"You look cute," she replied. "That dress suits a thin person."

In addition to the new dress, I had — miracle of miracles — long fingernails! For some reason, I quit biting my nails when I was in the hospital. My nails had been growing for three whole weeks and were almost a quarter of an inch long.

"I didn't know you even liked Eddie," Gretchen said Saturday morning on the phone. She was home on weekends, now that she and Doug weren't seeing each other.

"He's always been sort of a friend. But when he came to visit me in the hospital and brought me those awful flowers — okay, so he's not gorgeous like T.E. — "

"Don't put him down, Kobie, like you're always doing yourself. Eddie is a nice guy. Have a great time this afternoon. Don't forget to call me as soon as you get back." I couldn't detect a shred of resentment in

Gretchen's tone. She was sitting home alone these days, but seemed genuinely glad for me.

Eddie and his father arrived at exactly two-thirty. They were so punctual I wondered if they had spent the night in the bushes outside the front door until it was time to knock. My mother talked to Mr. Showalter, a plumper, older edition of Eddie, while Eddie and I looked at the floor and out the window and finally at each other.

For the occasion, Eddie wore a white shirt under his inevitable blue sweater and had squeezed himself into a new pair of Levi's, at least a size too small. He seemed so uneasy I couldn't decide whether he was nervous about our date or suffering from acute waistband.

I was nervous enough for both of us. After my mother had extracted a promise from Mr. Showalter that they would have me back *by dark*, Eddie took me out to his father's car. Our hands grazed. My palms were so clammy he must have felt like he was touching a dead mackerel. We got in the backseat with Mr. Showalter in the driver's seat, like a chauffeur.

The matinee crowd at the movie theater consisted of hollering little kids with their parents and Eddie and me. Mr. Showalter discreetly sat on the other side of the theater, stoically eating popcorn, while toddlers raced up and down the aisles and poured grape soda on his shoes.

Eddie bought a box of popcorn the approximate dimensions of a laundry basket and set it on the armrest between us.

"I got extra butter," he said.

My first date was only about thirty-seven minutes old and already I had to register a complaint. "Eddie, I love popcorn, but I can't eat it." All I needed was to get a popcorn hull stuck in my stupid throat.

"Oh, that's right!" He smacked his forehead. "I forgot. Would you like something else? Jujubes or something?"

"No, I'm fine. Can you eat all that by yourself?" I worried he would feel compelled to gobble the whole box and make the waistband of his jeans even tighter.

Then the lights dimmed and I was consumed with a new panic. The theater was a place where a boy traditionally "made his move" on a girl. Which move would Eddie try? The old yawn-then-drape-the-arm-across-the-girl's-shoulder routine? Or the sly reach-for-the-popcorn-at-the-same-time-and-wind-up-holding-hands ploy?

I sat stiffly, staring straight ahead, every pore braced for the invasion. But then the feature started and, to my amazement, Eddie did nothing except watch the movie. After a few minutes, I relaxed and let myself enjoy the movie. *Fantasia* was so mesmerizing, our eyes never left the screen.

When the movie flickered to an end and the lights came up again, we walked out of the theater, jabbering excitedly about the great animation we had just seen. In fact, we forgot about Mr. Showalter completely until he came staggering out into daylight.

"Where to now?" he asked Eddie.

Eddie turned to me. "Is Dino's Den okay with you, Kobie?"

I had never eaten in Dino's Den, a restaurant in the basement of a nearby shopping center. Dino's Den was so dark, customers should have been supplied flashlights to find their tables. Eddie and I sat across from each other in a booth, while Mr. Showalter squinted at the menu at the only other available table, one right next to ours. He sat with his back to us to give us a little privacy, but his constant presence made me feel like we were being hounded by the Secret Service.

"I liked the 'Night on Bald Mountain' part the best," Eddie said, still discussing the movie.

"Me, too! Weren't those dancing trees neat? When I get home, I'm going to try to draw one," I said.

"Will you bring it to school when you're done?"

"Sure," I replied, flattered Eddie was so interested in my art projects. To muffle my confusion, I studied the menu.

"They've got terrific ice cream here."

I wrinkled my nose. "If I never see a dish of ice cream again, it'll be too soon."

"I keep forgetting. Well, have whatever you want," he offered.

"You know what I want?" For the first time in weeks I was *hungry*. "A hamburger! I'm starving for a hamburger!"

"Me, too." Eddie ordered us both cheeseburgers and onion rings to share. Beside us, Mr. Showalter had a cup of black coffee.

"I like your dress," Eddie said. "I like your other dress, too, but this one is prettier."

"What other dress?" Usually I wore skirts and blouses to school.

"The white one with all the lace."

So he had seen me on Valentine's Day, when I had foolishly tried to make Turquoise Eyes fall in love with me. I didn't say anything. Somehow I think Eddie knew about my crush on Mr. Brown, the way he had known of my tonsillitis.

Recalling the role I was playing that day, it dawned on me that I made a poor Juliet, mainly because I wasn't being myself. But weren't we all playing roles? Sandy, the romance coach, trying on different identities. Stuart, anxious to appear dashing for Rosemary Swan. Gretchen, eager to be half of a couple before she was a whole person. And me, wanting desperately to outdo Gretchen by landing an improbable boyfriend. Only Eddie Showalter played himself, wearing his blue sweater, doodling the White House and jets. Never pretending to be what he wasn't. Maybe Eddie knew where he fit in this world. I was starting to figure out what my part was.

We ate our hamburgers and talked some more about the movie and about art. I never had such a good time and I told Eddie as much when his father stopped the car in front of my house. I thanked his father and started to open the car door myself, but Eddie jumped out and sprinted around to my side.

"I'll walk you to the door," he said. I loved the attention. He made me feel special.

At my door, we stood awkwardly. I wondered if my mother had surveillance cameras installed while we were gone.

"I had a really nice time," I said again.

"So did I. You always make me laugh, just like at lunch. You know, Kobie, I think you're — " He paused, as if searching for the right words.

"Yes?" I said, ready to supply a dozen suggestions. You think I'm what? Enchanting? Ravishing? Bewitching?

" — swell," he finished on a note of triumph.

I weighed being called an "enchanting creature" in my daydreams against being called "swell" in real life and decided I'd settle for "swell" any day. "I guess I'd better go inside."

The Big Moment was here. Eddie hesitated a few seconds, glanced about nervously as if anticipating my mother to spring out of the rhododendrons, then kissed me, very fast, but definitely on the lips.

" 'Bye, Kobie," he said, reddening from the neck up, like mercury rising in a thermometer. "I'll call you."

I went into my house, my feet scarcely touching the floor.

My mother was reading and not hanging out the window, spying on us as I thought she'd be. "You look happy," she said.

I was supposed to call Gretchen immediately and fill her in on the details, but I wanted to relish my first date alone a while. I'd call her later.

"I am happy," I told my mother. And I was. Happy to be myself, at last.

About the Author

CANDICE F. RANSOM, who to this day is amazed she made it through her freshman year, lives in Centreville, Virginia, with her husband and black cat. She writes books for young people and enjoys going out to eat whenever she can. She is the author of *Thirteen* and *Fourteen and Holding*.